Novels by
E. RICHARD JOHNSON
available from IPL Library of Crime Classics®

SILVER STREET
MONGO'S BACK IN TOWN*
THE INSIDE MAN*
CAGE FIVE IS GOING TO BREAK*
THE GOD KEEPERS*
CASE LOAD – MAXIMUM*
THE JUDAS*
BLIND MAN'S BLUFF*

forthcoming

E. RICHARD JOHNSON
SILVER STREET

INTERNATIONAL POLYGONICS, LTD.
NEW YORK CITY

For Nancy Huheey
for her faith and encouragement

SILVER STREET

Copyright © 1968 by E. Richard Johnson
Cover: Copyright © 1988 by International Polygonics, Ltd.
Library of Congress Card Catalog No. 88-80761
ISBN 0-930330-78-1

Printed and manufactured in the United States of America
First IPL printing May 1988.
10 9 8 7 6 5 4 3 2 1

INTRODUCTION

I began writing *Silver Street* as a form of escape from the boredom of a prison cell, and to see if I could put the reality of the streets and the people I knew into a novel.

I entered prison on Christmas Eve 1964 after seven years of moving from city to city, one job ahead of the police. Faced with a long sentence, I began writing as a form of escape, an attempt to give myself a goal and a purpose. First I wrote articles about the outdoors — about fishing and hunting — remembrances of my childhood in northern Wisconsin. Those, along with fillers and short pieces for children's magazines, met with some success, so in 1968 I tried writing a mystery novel. After all, crime was something I knew, and from an afternoon on the prison yard, I could find enough story ideas to stay busy for a year. In *Silver Street* I wanted both the criminals and policemen to be real, criminals who a reader could understand and policemen who sometimes found it difficult to live up to the image of their jobs. Being objective with my characters was not difficult; I have known both criminals and cops that I liked and respected.

Through *Silver Street* I also learned that writing was hard work, but although it took six months to finish the manuscript, it was work I enjoyed. I was fortunate enough with that first novel to find an editor with patience, Joan Kahn of Harper & Row. With the first novel published, and later an Edgar Award, I was sure that writing was the best part of my life and what I wanted to do in the future.

Several mystery novels followed *Silver Street* between 1968 and 1973, and with each one I realized how little I knew about writing, and how very lucky I had been to have a first novel published. Unfortunately, success with writing can bring some very negative things into a person's life, and in my case they were things I was not prepared to deal with.

I became involved with drugs. I also made some very bad business decisions regarding my choice of agents. By 1974 I was spending more time with drugs and less time writing and the drugs had become more important. After a brief parole, I returned to prison in 1978. Though still an addict, I realized that while prison was the place I had become an addict, it was also where I could stop. By 1980 I knew I could remain drug free and I began to think of writing once more, starting again with outdoor articles and children's magazines. I began mystery writing again in 1985 and was fortunate enough to locate my original editor with the help of Hugh Abramson at IPL.

At present, my first new mystery — *Blind Man's Bluff* — will be published in December 1987 by St. Martin's Press. A second novel, *The Hands of Eddy Loyd*, will follow in '88. Both new novels are a continuation of the detective characters I began in *Silver Street*.

Perhaps best of all, I've now been drug free for seven years. Writing is still hard work for me. I believe it may be harder the second time around as I learn more about the craft. But with the support and encouragement of editors such as Joan Kahn and publishers like Hugh Abramson, I hope to provide the readers with more mystery novels from plots found on the prison yard.

E. Richard Johnson
Stillwater, Mn.
September 1987

Pox upon thee, little fellow,
creep and pimp, with stripe of yellow,
With thy frightened, shifty glance,
and thy trembling in thy stance.

Mind the alley's dark open mouth.
Mind the shadows leaning close.

Pay heed to soft careful sounds,
cautious footfalls on the ground.
Watch, and wait, and stink with fear,
for in the dark your killer's near.

—TRASHCAN O'TOOLE
The Strip, 1964

ONE

THE RAIN was cold and from the north. It was hail-edged as the wind blew it in slanting curtains over the stockyards to stir old stenches and wash them toward the river. It pelted hardened drops on the glassy surface of U.S. 28 and blew in gusts over the shack-studded flats between the river and Silver Street, where it painted the aging buildings of the slums a lead gray that was broken only by the red flicker of bar lights and the occasional yellow eyes of a passing car.

The pimp stood on the corner of Silver Street, near the Third Street bridge. There was almost no traffic. The trade on Silver Street was snug in the bars where the free-lance whores pulled in the customers and made it difficult for a pimp to make a buck. It was lousy weather to make a buck in, anyway.

His name was Willie Mack, and he was known as Willie the Wimp, the rich whores' pimp, among the fellowship because it was a fact that Willie had never brought his girls a trick that was worth more than five bucks, and that on a pay-day night. But if you considered the merchandise he had to pimp for, it was understandable. Willie dreamed of getting himself a real classy doll that would be worth fifty bucks a pop, forty for him and ten for her. He was a generous soul, Willie was. Willie thought he had one.

He was also wet, soggy wet, from the bottom of his two-dollar shoes to his knees, where the cheap plastic raincoat held off the water. It was a losing battle, for the rain trickled in a persistent stream off his hat and down the back of his neck each time he raised his head to watch an approaching car. Each time he noticed, with wistful eyes, the far-off light near the corner of Eleventh Street that marked his favorite bar.

No trade for a pimp in the rain, Willie thought. That's what they say. Willie pulled a damp cigarette from inside his jacket and wished he was in bed with his new whore. If you can't sell it—screw it. They said that too. It was a good idea. At least it was a good idea with this new one. Seventeen she was, and built like a dream. She'd bring that fifty-a-pop soon as he got her broke in. Maybe tonight. If that bastard would get here!

He shivered and tried to smoke the wet cigarette until the wind beat it into bitter shreds against his lips. As far as he could see down Silver the street was empty. True, what they say. Nobody out but him and the weirdos. The guy had to be a weirdo to make a date with a pimp like he was making a business deal or something instead of looking to get his sock wrung. What the hell did he say on the phone? "Want some young stuff"? "A girl just getting into the business"? That was a laugh; they start giving it away at twelve. Well, for fifty bucks he'd tell him she was a cherry, if the bastard would get there.

Man, Willie thought. The first big trick. Fifty for one of his girls. That would shut them up. Smart bastards; a million cities in the country and all the pimps seem to be on Silver Street. Pimps' Row, the bulls call it.

Plenty of trade, he told himself. Boat hands from the river, and with the soldiers coming in. God damn that rain! Showed what kind of a pimp he was, though. The others sent their girls down to the bus station on a night like this and stayed in the bars. Who makes money sitting on their ass? A man's got to get out and hustle for his girls. Girls? Jesus; three dogs. How the hell did I get stuck with them, anyway? A man could work with this new one, though. She was damn good, for a kid. Willie edged across the sidewalk to lean against the building.

Ten more minutes, mister, and I'm gone. Teach her some new stuff and the night won't be a total loss. One of the dogs might pick up a buck, anyway.

He glanced at his watch.

Eight to twelve, he thought. Eight minutes, mister, and you can shove the fifty. That stupid bim might let him talk her out of it, anyway. They all want to give it away.

He looked south down Silver Street and saw the car.

Willie walked to the curb. The car was coming slow, like the driver was reading street signs. Almost sure to be the trick, he thought. Goddamn weirdo in a new car. That's the kind that were a pain in the ass—can't crawl on and get it over with. Not them bastards. They got to be

3

different. Takes the girls too damn long with some of them. Well, weirdo, he thought, just don't mark her up and you can do it standing on your head if you want to.

Willie shook his head, showering water. Can't have her marked up! Not for a lousy fifty. He tried to peer through the rain-fogged windows as the car stopped at the curb beside him, then glanced quickly down the street. There was no one in sight. He opened the door and smiled into the car.

"Mr. Mack?" the driver asked. "I'm sorry I've kept you waiting."

"That's okay," Willie said, getting in. A blast of cold rain followed him.

Silently the trick pulled out onto the street again. "And how is business tonight, Mr. Mack?" He glanced at Willie and smiled.

Willie shrugged, watching the street. "Not much action," he said. "You're lucky. I got what you want. Like you said—young—and I just got her working." He watched the pale face under the hat. Trick. He'd be telling them the same thing next year. How the hell do they know how often she's been plugged? He reminded himself that he should get them all shots next week.

The trick smiled and drove until he reached U.S. 28, then right, and, a block and a half later, left, into the stockyards, stopping the car in the shadow of a building. "Now we can talk, Mr. Mack," he said. "I have to be very careful."

Willie smiled vaguely in the dark. Real weirdo, this one. He pulled the damp pack of cigarettes from his coat.

The trick held a match for him. "Like I said over the phone," he said softly, "I'm willing to pay well. It's just

4

that I like to know the men I do business with. Yours is a fascinating profession."

Willie dragged deep on the cigarette and let the smoke out slowly. "Never thought about it like that," he said. "But I guess it is a kind of profession, ain't it? You got to be on the ball to handle four women."

He sank back into the seat and puffed happily. Yeah, a business. He liked to talk about his whores. Regular stud, he was. Keeping four toeing the line. The trick probably couldn't handle the one he had at home. Knew he wasn't a vice cop the minute I laid eyes on him. Pale, sickly bastard.

"Four!" the trick said. "Are they all young?"

"Naw," Willie admitted. "Just this last one. She's worth more than fifty, but I figure to keep her for a few regular customers. You know, guys I can depend on to come around." He smiled at the trick. "That way they can train her like they want, and they don't have to worry about getting clap when they want some strange stuff."

The trick laughed shortly. "That seems to be a good arrangement. But what if this girl isn't interested?"

Willie grinned at him, his eyes bright. "Man! Like I said, she's my whore. She does like I say."

"Do they ever get out of line?" the trick wanted to know. "Say one didn't want to work any longer?"

One of them, huh? Willie thought. Got to talk about slapping one around before he can screw her. Jesus, what a guy's got to go through for a lousy fifty!

Willie rubbed his pointed jaw. "Sure," he said. "They get out of line once in a while. This bim, the one I got for you, she gave me some crap at first. Said she wasn't going to lay no barge hand like I wanted her to. The

5

bitch said he stank, how about that? Said he stank, and him a goddamn captain, too. Anyway, I punched her out and put the blocks to her. She likes it rough like that." Willie sighed. He liked it like that, too.

"Go on," the trick urged in the dark.

"That's the way to treat them, rough. Especially the young ones. They get some stupid ideas that a guy like me won't keep them if they act too eager. So I says, look, bitch, you're going to screw if I'm around or not, so you might as well get paid for it."

"I see," the trick said. "You charm them into sleeping with you and then put them on the street, so to speak."

"Yeah, you could say that," Willie said. "They need a man to look after them."

There was something strange in the trick's voice, and Willie realized that it was very dark where they were, and whereas he had nothing against weirdos, he would have liked to be somewhere else telling him what a lady-killer he was. He considered the promised fifty and went on: "What say I take you over there?"

"In a moment," the trick said. He took out his wallet, smiling in a thin way by the dash light. Willie watched the thin fingers brush past a thick wad of bills and extract a photo. The trick handed him the photo and asked: "Is she as nice as that?"

Willie squinted in the gloom. "Sure," he said. "Built better . . ." He looked up into the trick's eyes. He did not like the eyes. They were dark with flecks of yellow in them, like a cat's. Like a cat's, looking at a rat it had cornered. His dislike probably had its origin in the dark and the rain moaning against the car. That was his dislike. His fear came from the flat automatic in the trick's hand. It was pointed at his chest.

"Jesus, mister!" Willie said, staring at the photo in his trembling hand. "What is this?"

The trick held out his hand. "Give me the picture, Mr. Pimp," he said. "And turn around on the seat."

"Sure. Sure." Willie shivered and turned, pressing his forehead and palms against the window. His reflection stared back at him from the rain-fogged glass, the eyes wide with fear. Jesus, oh Jesus, Willie thought. What's he want?

He jerked and trembled as the trick's hand touched his back, the fingers pressing hard as they moved down. The bastard's queer! he thought. He's gonna feel me up!

"Wait a minute, mister," Willie said. "You got the wrong guy."

The trick laughed softly. "I know," he said, "but you're one."

The fingers had stopped just over the fifth rib in Willie's back. Willie's reflection in the window seemed to bulge as the trick put the knife in. Willie's mouth opened as if to speak, but no sound came. Only a bubble of blood appeared on the yellowed teeth. A bewildered look crept into Willie's eyes as he slid down against the door. He's killed me, he thought vaguely. The weirdo's killed me.

The trick shoved the blade deep, knowing where it was slashing inside. "You don't need to pimp anymore, you bastard. You don't have to keep any girls in line."

He shoved the blade until the hilt pressed against Willie's back and twisted it sharply. He left the blade in Willie to keep him from leaking on the floor and lit a cigarette before he started the car.

He smiled as he drove back toward Silver Street. He had killed again and it was good. They did not expect it here. It was very good that way. He glanced down at Willie. Too bad this one didn't recognize the girl. The trick wiped his sweating hands, one at a time, on the seat. No matter, the next one would, or maybe the next.

Later, the rain was colder. It washed the gray streets and filled the gutters as it ran off toward the flats. It reached up to Willie's ears as he lay with the stench of the stockyards, washing his mouth and rushing on, stained pink. Willie was very dead.

A whore found him two hours later and stole his wallet with its two dollars before, from the bar down near the corner of Eleventh Street, she called the police.

TWO

TONY LONTO was a homicide bull. When the phone rang beside his bed, he ignored it for perhaps fifteen seconds before he picked it up. He was not on the duty roster at headquarters. He picked it up because there was a fifty-fifty chance that it might be his girl. It was Lieutenant Jaworski. "Come on in, Lonto," he said.

Lonto's voice was thick through the wire. "What's up?"

"We got a corpse for you," Jaworski's heavy voice boomed. "I said to myself, who'd be best for a body on the Strip? And right away your name pops up. Get over to Third and Silver. They're waiting for you."

"Okay." Lonto sighed and dropped the phone back into

its cradle. You'd think I was the only homicide cop around, he thought. Four of us in homicide, but not when the body's Third Ward. Then it's Lonto. Lonto, go down and find out which of your old school chums did this one. Lonto, check out this stiff, he's in a room in your old neighborhood. It wasn't that people didn't kill each other in the other wards; they just killed each other at a faster rate by the river. And that happened to be the neighborhood Lonto grew up in.

He got out of bed hurriedly. Lonto had a feeling that he should transfer to a south-side station and get away from the Strip. There were other places in the city as bad, but none as familiar to him. The Strip began at U.S. 28, on the north edge of the city, and followed both sides of the river, its heart stretching six blocks deep on both banks, from the highway down to Sixty-first Street, where Davis Drive cut it off from downtown and the 300 block ran into Davis on the other side where the city got better.

Lonto snapped on his service revolver under his jacket and took his hat and raincoat from the closet. He could hear the dark cold rain beating against the apartment windows.

Crap, he thought. I join the force to get out of the Strip and where do I work? Pimps' Row! It's a hell of a life. He grinned and went out to his car.

In all truth, Lonto liked his job. He liked being a cop. But there were times when the Strip and Lieutenant Jaworski combined were fate giving him the finger a bit too hard. And liking his job had nothing to do with liking the Lieutenant. The way Lonto figured it, the Strip was as good a place as any hole to work in, because he knew it. It helped sometimes. It didn't help that Jaworski was a polack that liked polack cops, or Irish cops. He might

10

even smile favorably on a Spanish or a Negro cop. But he damn sure didn't like dago cops. Especially dago cops that came from the same neighborhood where a dago hood had shot him dead in the ass at the beginning of his career. Jaworski remembered that.

Lonto remembered, too, as he drove. Big Dutch Matteo had shot a rookie cop in the ass twenty years ago, he thought. And Jaworski still feels it pucker when he sees a dago. Lonto knew Jaworski was a good cop. But he sure was a bitch to work for. He was finding it hard to be a homicide dick and be treated like a Mafia member by the Lieutenant. It would maybe be a good idea to transfer.

It would be a good idea, yes. If you were not as bull-headed as Lonto, and if you happened not to think you were doing a fair job on the Strip which Lonto did.

It would *not* be a good idea if you knew the Strip is a real bitch to work but you understand why it is. You know that Pimps' Row and Jackson across the river are a cop's nightmare, a festering gash on the city's face that stinks of evil when you walk it on dark nights. When you walk it on a hot summer day, you know how it feels, like the pressing distrust and hate there are all for you as you pound the pitted sidewalks.

And if you are a cop named Lonto, you know that the evil is real, and the hate is there, because you once stood on the street corners with larceny on your mind on dark nights, and watched the beat cop pass with hate in your eyes on hot days. So why be a cop, then? How can a slum kid put on the shield he grew up hating?

That's easy. It happens when you are a slum kid who was lucky enough not to get caught stealing, or jack rolling, or moll buzzing, or whatever the hell you were taking

11

on-the-job training for as a punk kid. You see the knifings, the muggings, the whore beatings, and you see the knifers, the muggers, and the pimps get caught—not always, but you see some get caught. If you are a smart punk, you see and understand all these things, and you understand that someday you will be caught. So you look around and you choose the side that seems to have the odds in its favor. If you are lucky when you do this, you will still be in possession of a soft place inside when you make your choice.

That's how you become a cop if you are a slum kid. If you have an inside knowledge of how pimps, hoods, whores, and punks work, and why some of the things happen on the Strip as they do, you do not become a clerk. You become a cop. Like Lonto became a cop.

The Strip smelled of death tonight in the rain.

The blue of four raincoated bulls was gathered around the body lying with its head in the gutter. There were a few brave onlookers gathered on the wet sidewalk. The flasher on the parked prowl car stabbed color into the rain and reflected off the car's hood as Lonto parked into the curb.

He slammed the car door and walked over to the beat bulls. He was rather small for a detective. He wore his hat pulled low over his dark eyes, and walked as if he expected something to blow up. He gave the impression of a tight-wire ready to snap. His hair was hard black against a dark complexion, and there was a sharp look to the high cheekbones and nose and a hungry look about his thin lips.

"Who found the carcass?" he asked.

12

A beat bull nodded to the prowl car. "Violet; he's calling in."

"Let's take a look," Lonto said, and moved to the canvas-covered body. The nearest beat bull uncovered Willie to the rain and studied Lonto. Lonto was a familiar face to the bulls, a homicide dick who could walk up on a patrolman taking a warming nip and act blind, or have one himself. A thirty-two-year-old dick who thought rookies should have, and be allowed, the same vices as the headquarters bunch.

So the beat bulls did not begrudge Lonto his still-dry shoes as they squished around the body, and the brief smiles on their faces were not automatic.

"Looks like a shiv job," the bull holding the canvas said. "One time."

Lonto grunted and knelt, fingering the two-inch cut in the plastic raincoat. "You turn him over yet?"

"Hell, no! He's just like they found him."

"I don't suppose the photographers have been here yet?" Lonto asked. He took a flashlight and went down on his knee to look at the face.

"Nobody's showed but you, so far."

"Okay, cover him up," Lonto said, getting up and walking to the prowl car. He opened the door as Patrolman Violet was hanging up the mike.

"Hi, Tony," Violet said. "You got this one?"

"Naw, I came down to visit. Fill me in, will you, Ed?" Lonto put an arm over the back rest and let the door close behind him.

Ed Violet was a barrel-bellied man with a thick mouth and heavy jowls. His hat and jacket were soggy. He was an old-time cop, but one out of the gravy beats. Residen-

13

tial beats, where a major crime was likely to be a quart of milk stolen off the back porch. Violet did not like being transferred to where blood came with crime. But he wore his cop's look and tried to hide what he felt.

He pointed to his own left chest. "Shiv in the heart. Looks like from the back," he said slowly. "One time."

"You find him cruising?"

"No. I was over on Olson, spotlighting the warehouses, Tony. Switchboard sent me over here to check out a report on a zombie blocking the gutter. They said a woman reported it. I found him like you see him, and nary a soul in sight. The rain's got the streets deserted, anyway."

"How about the woman who called?"

"The usual. A fast tip with no name attached." He nodded to another car pulling up in front of the prowl car. "We'll know who he is maybe when they get done with his screen test. Going out?"

Lonto shook his head. "Wet out there. We got time after they take the position shots."

Violet stared out the rain-streaked window. "Why don't they kill each other on nice nights?"

Lonto grunted and said nothing. He had visited other corpses in the rain. He had no intention of standing out in it to watch police routine, and maybe getting in the way. When he did get out, there was the usual crowd, swearing at the weather, but nobody was inclined to remain long after his job was finished.

The meat wagon was waiting with open doors when he helped the Doc roll Willie over. "Like I said," Violet spoke behind him, "looks like one wound."

"Maybe," Lonto said. He touched the raincoat. "We don't know what's under this. I've seen them shot two or three times and then dressed before they're dumped."

He turned to the Doc. "Open his mouth, will you?"

The Doc did, and looked with a flashlight. "You intend to do an autopsy here?"

There was a hardness in Lonto's voice. It came from an old blunder he'd made by calling a corpse a suicide when the man had died from an ice pick through the roof of the mouth. A fact that was made painfully clear by Lieutenant Jaworski. Lonto tried not to make the same mistakes twice.

"He's leaking from the mouth," he said. "I want to know why. He's been here quite a while, you know."

The Doc switched off the flash. "No wound inside. Now, I suppose you're going to tell me that means he's got a chest full of blood. I get all kinds of advice from you experts."

"I'll read your report," Lonto said, pulling up the sleeve to look at the thin arm.

"Junkie?" Violet asked.

"Don't look like it. He never was, though," Lonto said. He began going through the pockets.

Violet thought it over before he carefully asked, "How do you know he never was? He could be shooting any-place."

"Sure, he could," Lonto grunted. "He could be a sniffer, too. But he's not. He's a spongehead."

Violet got down and studied Willie carefully as Lonto's mouth spread into a grin. "Spongehead? What the hell says he's a spongehead?"

Lonto held the collection of junk he'd taken from the pockets, sorted it through and handed it to the Doc. "Keys, lighter, and twelve cents," he said. "Last of the high rollers he was."

"Why a spongehead?" Violet demanded.

15

"Shrewd detection, careful observation of the body, and many hours of study." Lonto kept it straight, serious as death as he stood up. "I think maybe recognizing him helped, too."

Violet blinked and stared at the grinning beat bulls making like dark avengers on the sidewalk. "You couldn't have just came out and said that, could you?"

"Nobody asked." Lonto nodded that he was finished to the Doc and smiled. "Wasn't sure until we flopped him, anyway. He's Willie Mack. A pimp. I think you should call in and have them pull the file on Willie. He's got two or three girls working, and I think they'll still be working yet. See if the vice squad has their addresses, will you?"

Violet started for the prowl car. "You thinking one of them made the call?"

Lonto watched the meat wagon's doors close behind Willie. He shrugged. "Maybe they'll tell us." He nodded at the beat bulls and started for his car, stopped, and said, "Tell Jaworski I'll be in shortly." He glanced at his watch. It was a quarter to two. "I'm going to eat."

It was one of those cases that he wished wouldn't start. They were the bad ones. The ones that hung in his mind after they were finished, if they ever were, because he knew some of the people involved. Lonto took out a cigarette and lit it. He was wearing a navy-blue suit and the new shoes he'd bought the previous day. He was going to pay for them again today. He realized that when he'd felt the water seeping inside. It was going to be a long day, on new, wet, and too-damn-tight shoes.

He swung the car into a hissing U-turn and drove back down Silver Street. I should ask for a partner on this one, he thought. There was too much to do already and

I've got a backlog. Check on the whores for a start. That will be a mess. Who'd want to kill a pimp, anyway? Balls! Dozens of people! Why can't I get a case where the carcass has only one, just one other person who'd like to see it a carcass? There is no such person, Lonto, so go feed your face and pick up the names of the whores.

He smiled briefly. Anna Ryan might not approve of such a pastime. But then it was too soon to be sure just how she felt about how Detective First Grade Tony Lonto spent his time. There was a great deal of difference between sleeping with a woman and knowing exactly how she felt about him. At least with Anna there was. During the six months he had dated her, he had managed to conclude the evening in bed only twice.

He had to admit that it was not an impressive seduction score. But there was no girl he'd rather be trying to seduce than Anna. She was certainly the most interesting and beautiful woman he had ever met. Her hair was copper blond. It was naturally that kind of blond, a fact that Lonto could swear to, but wouldn't. Her eyes were a light green and she had a deep lovely tan over her high-breasted body. Her face was rigged with changeable beauty and warm promise in the delicate features. Her lips were everything—full and soft, yet firm with a spice coolness—and she was everything Lonto had looked for from the Strip to Seoul and back again. He had found her exactly one hundred and eighty-two days ago, and he did not know a thing about her, except that she was a receptionist for a downtown business and worked almost as bad hours as he did. She lived alone and was keeping him in a state of perpetual wonder. That is, Lonto wondered when he was not with her. When he was, he didn't care. It always seemed like a large miracle that she was there. She was a dream that Lonto was frightened would vanish before he could talk her into being Mrs. Lonto, and raising blond, dago kids. It was an awesome thing to happen to a tough punk kid from the Strip who had liked nothing in his life but a battle-scarred alley cat that had picked his room in a six-story walk-up to bunk in. The cat had accepted the room's occupant with cool disdain. Lonto respected that cat like he could respect a derelict that crawled out of a shack on the flats by the river and took time to wash his face with a filthy handkerchief before he went off to panhandle two bits for a glass of wine. There was a certain dignity in the cat and a vague resemblance to a human being in the derelict.

A resemblance that was as hard to find on the flats as a virgin was on Pimps' Row. Being a cop didn't help you find either one. It seemed that whenever Lonto worked on the Strip, everybody knew him, like he was wearing a sign that said: "I'm a cop! Dummy up!" But when he happened to visit, nobody knew him, like he'd died when he joined the force. And the Strip didn't change, you only saw it from a different view. The fun rumbles between block gangs turned into bloody, gut-spilling riots. There had been two already during the summer with a hot August yet to go.

The boosting in department stores, and peddling the boosted goodies, led to slow-paying fences. Which led to enforced payment with broken heads or dead fences, and this accepted practice was now viewed as homicide from Lonto's new position.

The pushers contributed their bit also. Everybody knew that they cut the stuff they sold so they would have more to sell. And so the addicts had to buy more, to keep the wiggly horrors from crawling around in their minds. So

18

they stole more, and fenced more, to slow-paying fences.

And cold bodies turned up regularly.

And, now, the pimps had contributed to Lonto's chosen view of the Strip again. A pimp usually does not turn up dead in the gutter. The whores do more often. A pimp is a thinker, not a doer. He directs the action, and, if anyone gets butchered, it is usually the whore who had twitched forth to do his bidding.

That is how it usually happened. It was not how Willie Mack had happened. It bothered Lonto. A pimp could be done in by one of his girls who could be motivated by money, love, or just for the hell of it. That was an accepted form of pimp killing. Or another pimp could do him in over a sweet little money-maker that they both wanted to sell and sample. In that case, there would have been a whisper passed to the cops about the coming event, because there is nothing that can match a good pimp fight, with all the whores cheering them on. And the last popular motive for doing in a pimp occurred when the pimp tried his hand at blackmailing a trick.

All these popular motives were a pain in the ass to Lonto. Not because he didn't appreciate having a good motive to work with. He simply knew that a pimp led a screwed-up life, and that it was going to be a long, hot day untangling some of it.

So when Lonto drove down Silver Street Tuesday morning, he let himself think about the few nice things he had to feel good about. Like Anna. And the fact that he was on homicide detail instead of the vice squad. Worse yet, on the fairy killer detail of the vice squad, where all you did was stand around the toilet at the bus station with your jock out and acted like you were taking a leak, while all the time you were waiting for someone to grab your jock, so you could pinch him for grabbing the jock you'd been dangling out for the past two hours. Even if you just drilled a hole in the wall and watched for jock grabbers, it was one hell of a detail.

He thought about it all: Jaworski—working the old neighborhood—a dead pimp in the rain. Lonto liked his work; he liked to think that being there working helped keep, in a small way, nice things like Anna from seeing an ugly part of the city. All that the cops did—lying a little, covering a little, hushing it up a little—helped keep the ugly facts from jumping up and hitting people like Anna in the face. That was another reason that Lonto was a cop, he didn't like the things that he knew were in the city.

The rain was piddling to a reluctant stop when he parked the car in front of the all-night diner by the station house.

THREE

ANNA RYAN watched the piddling rain from a bedside
window. Beyond the dark bulk of buildings she could see
the faint gray of dawn in the sky. It was not her apartment; it was a downtown hotel room. It was never her
apartment, except when it was Tony Lonto she was in
bed with. The man beside her on the bed was the usual
trick for Anna to be in bed with. He was old, with false
teeth, and tired out. But he had got his hundred bucks'
worth, the hundred he had given Anna when she had
arrived for their date.

There was an unconcealed venom in her eyes as she
stared at the sagging flesh on the man's face, and the

balding head resting on the pillow near her shoulder. A date, he had called it, Anna thought. They can't just admit that they hired you to screw. They want to call it intercourse instead. And they want to slobber on your mouth and bite your neck while they expect you to enjoy it, when all they're paying for is your box. God, they make me sick.

What was there about her that made it so repulsive now at a hundred bucks a pop, when it hadn't been a twenty dollar amateur harlotry? Now only with Tony was it any good. She had certainly played it straight as a virgin with him, and with no payment for that. Catch that good-looking cop paying for a roll in the hay! She would have to tell him. Just that she was a call girl—a high-class whore to a cop. She wouldn't lie to him any longer. He was a cop, for God's sake. He would understand. At least he might, if she waited a little longer. If he loved her. If he loved her he'd understand it all.

But Anna couldn't understand. Not even that first time which was the second, really. The first time had been fumbling, painful, and rather messy. But the second time it had been with a man, not the boy from across the hall. She'd felt the fever grow inside her that second time. The wild desire started that had never been totally quieted since. And the man had paid her two dollars. Five, the next time she had skipped school to go with him to that shabby apartment that hadn't been shabby then.

She began to feel the heat rise inside her. She shook her head and glanced at the sleeping hulk beside her. Wake up, she thought. I'll give you a bonus. She turned toward the window again. He would be as useless as he'd been last night, a spent weight, while the heat inside her still burned hot enough to make her feel dirty.

It had been better when she was eighteen and the men

22

were young, with thin wallets and hard bodies. Bodies that almost, but not quite, quenched the heat. And never coming close enough to doing that to make her stop selling it for the security of a wedding band, though there had been plenty of offers from men with scratched backs and hopeful eyes.

Anna was a fortunate whore, or an unfortunate one, depending on how you looked at it. She had never allowed booze or dope to control her body. But it was her body that controlled her. Anna had long ago decided that since she was cursed with an apparently incurable case of hot pants, she would collect a fee while she searched for a cure. There was, she'd realized, a large supply of willing men that were eager to satisfy her superb body. And willing to pay while they tried to. It was a much better arrangement than giving it away.

The only man she had given it to was Tony Lonto, who didn't know there was a price tag on what he was getting, and went ahead and left her feeling complete in the morning.

These days Anna had such a good pimp that all her dates were a hundred dollars a pop. And like the man beside her, they gave her nothing except the hundred, which she split with her pimp. Anna's dates ranged from wealthy businessmen to the top brass from the army base. She was a high-class whore, with a high-class pimp that knew a lot of important men, men with money. Anna had never propositioned a man since she had walked into her pimp's bar on Silver Street. He was at the bar, dressed well, considering the place, and Anna was looking for money rather than a cure that day because she had just arrived in town, leaving the last one a jump ahead of the vice bulls.

"You got too much class for the Strip, baby," he had

said, looking her over. "I got just the place for you."

"You mean you'd like to handle the merchandise?" she'd asked.

"Yeah," he'd said. "I get samples and half. Hundred-buck tricks, kid. You're too much to waste down here."

He found her an apartment uptown, away from the Strip, and took his samples before he started sending her out on dates. He was the best pimp Anna had found. And it was necessary to have a pimp in a new town. When she operated with her pimp, she had little to worry about from the vice squad, and all the risks of picking up trade on the street were eliminated. Anna's prices were as high as she'd ever had them, and that made her pimp happy. Only it did not make Anna happy. She stayed completely and totally unhappy until Tony Lonto turned up in her life and stilled the fire in her loins.

In a way, Anna had been trying on shoes all her twenty-seven years, and had finally found a pair that fit her. She would be willing to raise blond dago kids to keep them. But there was a catch. The catch would come by later today and pick up his fifty dollars. Her body, and sweet innocent looks, had gotten her into as fine a mess as heroin or booze had ever gotten a whore. She had found her cure for her body in Lonto, who happened to be a cop, but she also had a growing business with her other man, who happened to be a pimp, a high-class pimp, but one that would do the same thing to her as a low-class pimp would if she stopped selling it and making money for him. Her pimp would not like her giving it to one man who would in all probability keep her pregnant, in housedresses, and worrying about how to live on a detective's pay. That is why Anna had not tested the subject with either of them. That is also why she had gone

24

to bed with Lonto only twice, because she had promised herself that the third time she would tell him some things about Anna Ryan that would surprise him.

She was dressing when the man awoke. Even in his numb state he felt self-conscious about having fallen asleep with a woman he'd paid for. The old ones were like that. They hated to admit they were old.

"Leaving already?" he asked her.

"Unless you have other ideas."

"Oh, God, not now. That's all I have, ideas. Getting old, I guess." He said it matter-of-factly and waited, watching her.

"You're great," she finally said, "better than most." And they're mostly useless at your age, she thought. Her praise for his bed manners was part of why Anna was in demand.

"I'd like to get my money's worth," he said, smiling. "But I'm just too bushed. I'm afraid I'm not as good now as I was at nineteen."

"You're still a prince."

He glanced at his watch and said, "It's still night, hardly four-thirty."

She shrugged. "Would you like me to come back to bed?" she asked. "You know, finish my shift?"

He looked at her curiously, sitting up. His daughter was about the same age. "Will I see you again?"

"All you have to do is call Nicholas," she said. "That's the only way."

"I didn't mean that way," he said. "I dislike dealing with a common pimp."

Anna cased the soft swell of her breasts and stood facing him in panties and halter. "But you don't mind dealing with a common whore, is that it?"

"I didn't mean it that way," he said hurriedly. "You're terrific, absolutely great. That sweet body of yours makes me feel like someone pulled my backbone out. I thought we might make a more permanent arrangement."

She walked slowly over to the bed, pressed his face against the soft swell of her belly, and felt the fever start along with the hate inside her. She stared down at his balding head. "It can be as permanent as you like," she said, hating him because he did not pull her eagerly down or respond other than to run his hands over the soft skin of her back. "As often as you like. All you have to do is call Nicholas."

"Do you love him?"

She laughed and pulled away, picking up her dress. "That's a vulgar expression. Like asking you if you love your vice-president. Just because a woman has a pimp, as you say, doesn't mean she can't get along without one." She smiled. "He is very handy though. I wouldn't have met you if it weren't for him. You'd hardly try to pick me up on the street, would you?"

She looked with concealed distaste at the blue veins on his hands as he reached for a cigarette. "No, I suppose not," he said. "It amuses me to think I would have mistaken you for an attractive housewife."

She looked at him with a blank expression and finished dressing before she said, "I'll play house with you anytime you call."

"Call Nicholas you mean?"

"Yes, call Nicholas." She went to the bathroom and gathered up her things. She paused at the hall door. "Don't keep me waiting too long," she said, and went out.

"Cheap bitch," he said aloud after she'd gone. He settled back in bed and remembered he was expected home that night. P.T.A. meeting or some damn thing.

And Anna, calling a cab from the phone booth on the sidewalk outside, thought about the five twenties in her purse. Cheap bastard, she thought. Not even a tip. She glanced at a slow-moving prowl car crossing the intersection, and her heart pounded a moment before she realized that she was far from Lonto's duty area, and there was little chance of his riding a prowl car around town. She became a bit frightened when she thought about his finding out before she had found enough nerve to tell him, and she could not decide just what to tell her pimp yet.

"Tell him to look on the bulletin board," the desk sergeant was saying when Lonto walked into the station house. "It's right there in the squad room. Patrolman Violet, to Detective Third. Soon as he gets in, we hit him to stand coffee around, and then he gets his ass on the detective detail."

Lonto stopped at the desk and nodded to the two rookies talking to Sergeant Wolverton. "One of Jaworski's favorites, Sarge? A promotion, and a double shift to go with it?"

"Remember yours?" Wolverton asked, and looked at the two rookies. "He came off a fifty-hour run with the robbery detail, and the Lieutenant sent him a first-grade slip and put him on a murder. Went close to eighty hours on naps, didn't you, Tony?"

"Yeah," Lonto said. "Slept four hours and went another forty after that. The Lieutenant believes in getting forty hours' work out of every twenty-four."

"Ain't it the truth!" Wolverton said, and pointed an

ink-smeared finger at the two retreating rookies. "Not like they used to be, Tony. Time was when a cop expected to work fourteen-hour shifts."

"How's business?" Lonto asked, not wanting to hear about the good old days again.

Wolverton was what happens to a good many cops who give up and just play it for existence. He was about forty-six years old, with a dead face that revealed nothing and an attitude that pretended total disassociation from humanity. He was full of hurt. His eyes were red with sleeplessness and his mind was packed with memories of baby rapers, axe killers, and a generous assortment of how *dead* fourteen-year-old punks could make a cop or another fourteen-year-old punk. He longed for his pension and retirement when he could forget all the years of being a cop.

"Business is good as usual," he said. "What would you like, burglars, an attempted rape, a mugger? The cells upstairs are almost full. There's even a nice young man up there who spent the night cutting his mother up with a broken whisky bottle. She's over at General, getting sewed up and saying he didn't do it, or mean to do it."

"They never mean it," Lonto said. "Did the vice squad drop off a file for me?"

"In on your desk," Wolverton said. "I'll send in the autopsy as soon as it comes."

"I'll go down," Lonto said. "They write in code, and I wind up going down, anyway. I can't figure out why they can't just say a body had its guts spilled by a razor, or a sharp knife, instead of sending over a five-page report on the names of the intestines he managed to tangle around his legs before he laid down and died."

"Still hot about that one, huh?" Wolverton asked.

"You're still soft, Tony. You ain't hot at the lab boys; you're hot because it happened, and he was alive enough to walk them out for you to see."

"Violet made it, huh?" Lonto said, changing the subject. "I hope the Lieutenant puts him in homicide. We sure as hell need some more men."

"This goddamn station has always needed men," Wolverton said. "I've never seen it up to what we should have."

"We should have a lot of things," Lonto said, and headed for the four-desk office that the homicide detail called home.

The two main things he should have just then, as he saw it, were a wife, and a killer to give Jaworski. All in due time, he thought, when he reached his desk. He glared at the typewriter before feeding a piece of paper into it and opening his notebook. In order to be a cop, he had to make reports. He hated typing reports almost as bad as reading autopsies and other cops' reports.

At 7:00 A.M. he had finished with the vice squad's report on Willie Mack. And he knew why he hated reading the reports so much.

FOUR

THE VICE SQUAD's report had told Lonto that Willie Mack had three whores, each with a rap sheet as long as your arm. It was from the last of these three that he got the name of Helen Morafka, who was as yet unknown to the vice squad and was Willie's newest whore. The name was the only useful advice he had received from the uncooperative whores, who were more interested in finding another hard-up pimp to take them on than they were in helping the cops find out who had stuck a knife in their last one.

So Lonto was resenting uncooperative whores in general, along with his new shoes that were pinching hell out of his feet, when he climbed up three flights of stairs to knock on the door of Helen Morafka's room.

He was about to knock for the third time, when she opened it. She was a small girl, with dark eyes and hair, and firm breasts that stuck straight out against the thin housecoat she wore. Her eyes were tired and the face looked that way, too, because it was too early for make-up.

"Yes?" she asked.

"Miss Morafka?" Lonto asked, and waited until she nodded before he flashed the panic button. "I want to ask you some questions about Willie Mack."

"I don't know anyone by that name," she said, holding the door.

"Don't play games with me," Lonto said. "Willie's a pimp, and you're one of his hookers. Trixie, they call you. We can do it here or down at the station."

"What about Willie?" she said.

"Let's talk inside."

Trixie held the door open. The room was very small, decorated in Early American Slum style, with an iron frame bed that matched the cracked plaster on the walls, and the blackened hot plate sitting on a card table by the window. There was a chair, a dresser with a cracked mirror above it, and a yellowed sink with a cold-water tap.

Lonto took the chair and sat facing Trixie on the bed. She held the housecoat closed with one hand, and brushed at her hair with the other.

"Okay, so I know Willie," she said.

"Knew," Lonto told her. "He's down at the ice house on a slab. You knew that, didn't you?"

"I heard," Trixie said. "What's that got to do with me? I was here all night."

"How long has he been pimping for you?"

"He wasn't. I mean he'd just started. I only met him a couple of weeks ago."

"How old are you, anyway?"

She crossed her legs. "Old enough. What's that got to do with Willie?"

"I'd find out if I pulled you in, Trixie."

"Eighteen," she lied.

"How long have you been selling it?"

"What are you, a vice cop?" she wanted to know. "I was giving it away in grade school. What's the difference if I get paid for it?"

"None, I guess. How'd you get tied up with Willie?"

"He had a place to sleep when I needed one. I gave him a little for it. He wasn't hard to please."

"And?"

"And he liked what I had. He said he could get me some good tricks. You know."

"So he put you on the streets," Lonto said. "When did you last see him?"

Trixie kept forgetting to hold the housecoat, which kept falling open. She frowned. "About eleven-thirty last night. He came up here to tell me that he was bringing a trick up. I didn't go out because of the rain."

"Who was the trick?"

"I don't know." She paused. "You know better than that, cop."

"Who was the trick?" Lonto growled.

"Oh, shit. I don't know, anyway. You think I check their driver's license when they come up here? They didn't show up, so I went to bed."

32

"They?"

"Willie said he was bringing him up."

Lonto studied her face. "Why should he bring a trick up? All he had to do was send him."

"Why don't you leave me alone?" she asked. "How should I know why he was bringing him up? All I was supposed to do was go to bed with him."

"Answer my questions and I'll leave you alone," Lonto said. "Just tell me what Willie said when he came up here. Did this guy want some special treatment?"

"I'm a straight girl, mister," she flared.

"Or was he a regular?"

"Listen, all he told me was he'd gotten a call down at Frenchie's, the bar on Eleventh, and this guy is going to pick him up before they come up here. Now why don't you get to hell out of here?"

She's got to be hard, Lonto thought. She's got to be a hard ass and hate cops, or she won't have the guts to go looking for a trick tonight so she can eat tomorrow. And she just doesn't know how to bring it off yet.

She looked very frightened to Lonto, and this he could understand. It was perhaps her first time to be faced with a cop that could take her down and let the vice squad make a jacket on her. One that would follow her the rest of her life. A paper judas tag that could finger her as a whore for the rest of her life. But Lonto could do nothing about that. All he could do was try to get the answers he needed. The fact that Trixie was scared might help.

"All right, listen to me," he said, taking out his notebook that had nothing at all on Trixie in it. "You want to be cute about this, and I've got enough here to get you six months on the farm with the rest of the whores. I'll get to hell out, all right, and we'll both go down to the station. You wouldn't be the first hooker around here that we slapped a V.D. tag on and sent out for a cure."

"I don't have . . ."

"How the hell do you know?" Lonto smiled. "If the Doc says you got it—you got it. Our Doc, that is."

"Look, mister. Why should I lie to you? I just don't *know* who Willie was bringing up here."

"He do a lot of business from Labiche's bar?"

Trixie seemed surprised. "You know the place?"

"I know the place. Now, did he?"

"It was one of his favorite spots, I guess," she said. "You're not going to take me in, are you? I mean like you said?"

Lonto grunted and kept looking at his notebook. "You know of anyone that Willie was afraid of? Any trouble lately?"

"No."

Lonto tapped the notebook on his knee and looked closely at the girl. Unless she was lying, her story made the trick a very interesting man, but it was just as likely that Willie had been found by a mugger before the trick showed. That was one of the troubles with a body on the Strip. You could never be sure how much scavenger work had been done on it before the police were called. Lonto also knew that there was a less than even chance of finding a killer in the backwash of Silver Street. There were too many potential ones. Too many there that would kill for a fin or for fun, and sometimes did. He knew, too, that if the case found its way into the back of the unsolved files, nobody was going to raise a stink. So a pimp got killed. So what? Who gives a shit? Just go out there and protect the taxpayers. It was a lousy situation.

Trixie was a lousy situation. By rights, he should run her down to the station house and let the vice boys put her picture in their book. Only it wouldn't make her stop selling it, or make her get her shots any more regularly. He didn't have the faintest idea what would make her do that.

"How about it, mister?" Trixie asked. "I could maybe help you forget about taking me in. Some cops take a little trade."

The housecoat was open and Lonto enjoyed the view. She was very nice, and it seemed like a damned waste. "Cover it up, kid," he said. "I'm not looking for any free hump."

He smiled at her and wrote for a moment, then he tore out the sheet. "You call me if you remember anything," he said, knowing she wouldn't. "The other address is a coffee shop over by the station."

He shoved the notebook into his pocket and walked to the door, feeling like an ass as he always did when he did something useless. "The coffee shop's looking for a girl," he said, and went out feeling her eyes on his back. What the hell do you say to an eighteen-year-old whore?

It had been a long time since he'd tried to give advice, such as it was, to anyone. Besides the fact that nobody took it, people resented any advice until they got tossed into the slammer and if they did or didn't resent it then it didn't matter as much as a scab on a derelict's ass. You didn't try to tell the old ones, but once in a while a man did a stupid thing and tried to help a young one. And the next time he saw Trixie on the Strip would be soon enough to tell the vice squad that there was a new headache on the street.

Among the old headaches on the Strip was Frenchie Labiche's bar, just off the corner of Silver Street and Eleventh. Lonto parked across from it and watched while he smoked.

It was one of the older buildings on the street. Silver Street was all old, from the highway down to Davis, but Frenchie's was one of the oldest, a firetrap among firetraps. While the bigwigs and landlords that owned the rest of the Strip stayed out of it, Frenchie Labiche operated his holdings.

And here I am doing the old Silver Street bit again, Lonto thought. Ah, that's right. You! The junkie holding up the pool hall's window. You're not very high, are you? Fish-eyed me for a cop as soon as I parked. What's the matter, junkie? Do I look green to you? Does this suit look like a Gestapo uniform? Why the fish-eye, junkie? I could be coming down here tomorrow to find out who put a shiv into you. Going to spread the word, huh, junkie? Flatfoot outside? Sure you are.

Ah, but there's a hooker by the newsstand who's picked up your stare, junkie. Are you people telepathic? Or, maybe I smell like a cop now. I've got a surprise for you, though, junkie. You too, whore. This is little Anthony Lonto, top shiv of the River Hawks, dropping in to see the old gang. Remember little Anthony? Mean little son-of-a-bitch, wasn't he? Everybody said he'd be big-time someday. What happened? Oh, he figured he'd do a short tour in a place called Korea, yeah, like gonorrhea, a place he wanted to visit because he was tired of the stink down here. Damned if it didn't stink worse there. Stank so bad of fear and death that little Anthony would have been glad to be back here.

We had some dandy rumbles over there, just like back here. And that's what happened to Anthony Lonto, see? He got a bellyful. He wanted to crawl off someplace where it wasn't quite so rough, where the things didn't stink so bad, and the only place he could crawl to was here. Oh, yes, it still stinks here; you make it stink, junkie, you and the whore. But little Anthony don't. He walks in it, waters it down, and carries it around in his mind—compliments of one Lieutenant Jaworski. But he don't add to the stink. Hits you right in the crotch, huh? Well, that's the way it is, I guess. You'll just have to fish-eye me, and lie to me, because I'd ask to come down to this hole even if that bastard Jaworski didn't assign me. Because someone's got to do it, don't they? And who finds stink better than little Anthony Lonto? He understands how it's made.

Lonto knew who else made some of it. He tossed his cigarette out the window and got out of the car. He expected to learn exactly zero inside Frenchie's Bar. But you could never tell. He grinned and turned toward the newsstand on the corner. Some people like cops. Like Trashcan O'Toole who ran the newsstand. At least O'Toole would smile even if he hadn't picked up any news that would help.

O'Toole was a shriveled little man with a like for everybody and a morbid mind that made him bastardize poetry into monstrous verses about the Strip and the people there. He had a bad leg and a quick mind, and was reading a sports section inside the dim cubicle of his newsstand when Lonto leaned over the counter.

"Pssst," Lonto hissed. "Got any dirty pictures for sale?"

Without looking up, O'Toole laid the paper down. "You ain't fooling me into a frame, cop. I've been selling heat on this corner for twenty years, and there ain't a bunko dick around that can break my game."

"Going to be tough, huh?" Lonto said. "Well, you either come across with some graft, or I'll pinch you for climbing out of the sewer too early."

O'Toole grinned at the game, and rose holding out his hand. "Hi, Tony. How's my favorite cop? You down here on the Willie Mack business?"

"What else?" Lonto asked. "Always business down here. You pick up any whispers on it?"

"It's a surprise to us folks, Tony," O'Toole said, shaking his head. "Everybody's thinking he got mugged, but everybody knows that Willie didn't carry enough loot to get mugged for."

Lonto picked up a magazine and thumbed through it. "Nobody's got any ideas, then?"

O'Toole shrugged. "They got lots of ideas, all right, but they're out in the open with them, so they're just guessing like me. When someone knows something it'll come around quiet like."

Tony folded the magazine and put it into his pocket. Then he laid a ten on the counter. "You might see that I get it when it does get talked about," he said.

O'Toole dropped the ten into his apron. "Sure, Tony. I'll see what I can find out."

Tony liked the little man, which was something, because he did not particularly care for stoolies. But O'Toole didn't play stoolie for anyone but him, and then only when he was asked to. He didn't volunteer information on the people he lived with. O'Toole figured that Lonto was still a neighborhood kid.

O'Toole watched Lonto go down the sidewalk and turn into Frenchie's Bar. He's gonna get himself killed someday, O'Toole thought. Some punk's gonna kill him because he crawled out of here and he comes back to rub their noses in it.

FIVE

THE TRICK lay in bed and listened to the sound of the Strip waking up as the sun went down. The coming dark had always excited him. He could not say why, except that it was good to prowl in the dark black where no one could see. The dark brought out the people who would hurry from street light to street light, glancing warily at the shadows in the alleys and searching like moths for light. And the dark brought out the trick who padded from black alley to the black of a stairwell, always searching. He had never known what he had been searching for, really, until he'd found the pimp in the rain.

He was alive again, for the first time since the girl had

died. For the first time since they said he could not kill for them any longer and sent him home—to find her dead. But even if she had lived, she could not have stilled the excitement that the dark and the knife gave him. He had feared them at first, almost as though he knew they had always been what he looked for in his night's prowlings.

He smiled slowly into the growing dark, a feeling of expectancy creeping over him. He fumbled a cigarette from the pack on the night table and lit it, remembering the first one.

The jungle quiet had been huge, huge as death itself as they waited in the dark for them to come down the path. The knife was cold and wet with sweat in his hand, an untried fang. A remembered order was in his mind. You wait, you lie still like a rock, and you wait until they come to relieve the dead guard.

He remembered hearing them come, high singsong voices, muted to whispers, and how the knife had felt right then, as his hands had come up from the wet grass to grip startled flesh and he felt the solid jar of the bayonet slashing through the flesh of the back. He had twisted the blade, driving it deep as the warm pour of red crept over his cold hands. When it was done he knew that he no longer feared it. He felt the power in him and the knife, and he had volunteered for ambush patrols often after that to taste the power. There was no fear of war then, only a joy that he had never felt before. And he knew that he was one of those they talked about. The born killer, the man who killed as often in combat as he could, with sure precision, and no fear. The others had seen it, too, and they avoided him. Even the officers had seemed relieved when the orders had come to send him home.

But he had not gone home. He had come to the city, and found the girl dead, and the dark of the city filled with expectancy.

He slid silently out of bed and crossed the room to the window. Through the pale gray of dirt on the glass, he watched the dark creep along the street. It was fought weakly by the neon lights along the building fronts, like fireflies marking the heavy jungle air.

"Cecil?" Dora Valdez's voice was a sleepy question from the bed.

He faced her and smiled in the dark. "Time to get up," he said. "If you intend to work tonight."

"I have to," she said, in a slow voice. "I can't give it away to everyone and pay my rent."

"Pay *his* rent, you mean," Cecil said, walking back to the bed. He watched her sit up in a rustle of sheets. "That's what you mean, isn't it?"

The sound of the city was a low murmur creeping into the room. He could hear it calling from the dark. The white of the sheets was a pale vagueness under her shape. He leaned over and gripped her shoulders.

Dora reached up and pulled him down with her as she fell back. "Don't start that. Please, Cecil," she whispered against his chest. "Sometimes I wonder if that's not the only reason you come here. To get me for nothing, and cheat him. Like he was the one that put her . . ."

He laughed, covering her mouth with his lips. Then, "I come here for you. Forget about her, and her pimp. I have."

She looked up at his face. He was so young, ten years younger than her thirty years, and there was a strangeness in him that she did not understand. Not that she tried to, or really wanted to. Dora was a whore growing old at thirty, and she did not want to question what brought a young man to her bed. Knowing that he turned to her because she had known his girl before she'd hanged herself was enough. But she was curious.

"Have you?" she asked. "You make love like you're doing it for revenge."

He smiled and slipped a hand over her breast. "Trying to catch up on it. I've got thirty days to catch up on two years."

"You wasted some of it that first week, getting drunk," she said. "I didn't think you'd ever sober up."

The smile faded from his face. "So I got drunk when I heard. Did you expect me to take it with a smile when she wasn't honest enough to tell me about it? I would have understood, you know—she didn't need to kill herself."

She shook her head. "No," she said quickly. "I didn't want to bring that up. But I'm glad I told you about me before you came up here. You never know about you young ones. Some of them get so shook up when a girl takes them to bed that they figure they own her."

That's what she said, Cecil thought. "Do I own you?" he asked lightly.

"I wish you did," she said, and moved her hips under him. "But I have to take me out and make some money."

He could feel the excitement building in him, thinking about the dark waiting outside, and feeling her soft and warm under him. His hands found her long hair and pulled her head back so that her lips were under his. "After me," he said, forcing himself between her rising legs, and driving his eagerness into her as savagely as his pale hands drove the knife.

It was the first time he had mixed the dark expectancy

43

and her with the thought of the power that he held in his hands, and he was spent in moments. He rolled away and lay breathing heavily on the bed.

She turned toward him, fingers touching his shoulder. "God!" she said. "What got you so worked up? Like a rabbit that time."

He smiled into the pillow. "Good pussy," he said. "And I'm still catching up." He remained still under her hand, wanting her to leave. This was only part of his night, he thought. The best would be the knife.

Tony Lonto was goddamn sick of knives. He was sick of knives, and razors, and broken bottles that were used to spill someone's guts as neatly as an all-American gut ripper. He was sick of the day's heat and his sore feet. He was also tired of being lied to. He figured he had been lied to enough for one day.

He wanted to do nothing but go to his apartment, and call it a day. He certainly didn't want to top his day off with a visit to Lieutenant Jaworski. But he was on his way to do just that.

Okay, you polack son-of-a-bitch, he thought when he reached the office door. Now you can make my day complete.

He knocked on the frosted glass and waited until the deep voice said "Come on in" before he turned the knob and did.

Lieutenant Jaworski was the kind of cop who had gone in the hard way to make something out of himself against long odds. But everybody, be he a cop or a street sweeper or a millionaire or a derelict, is filled with a hunger, a doubt, or hurts somewhere. Being a good cop didn't stop Jaworski's ass from hurting when he saw a dago. He

44

knew it didn't hurt in his ass, it hurt in his mind. Getting shot in the ass had hurt his pride severely. Jaworski found it difficult to convince himself that it was all in his mind when Lonto was around. But he tried.

Jaworski's voice was like a rasp. He was a broad-shouldered, heavy man, like rookies had to be when he joined the force. His big face was lined with years of suspicion and resentment. He had a bald head and a pair of sharp blue eyes that peered at Lonto from under a pair of shaggy eyebrows.

He did not like Lonto, but he respected him. He respected him as a cop. He thought Lonto was one of his best cops, and that was the worst part of it. He needed cops like Lonto. So, he could not very well let that mental pain in the ass take away one of his good cops, no matter how much he'd like to see Lonto transfer.

"What have you got on this Mack case, Lonto?"

"Sore feet, a tired ass, and a hungry gut," Lonto said. He leaned against the wall across from Jaworski's desk and watched the glow of street lights coming on outside, and he thought about the people on the Strip.

"Boy, I see you're in your usual humor," Jaworski said. "Okay, okay. So it wasn't your shift. You're a cop twenty-four hours a day, remember?"

"How can I forget?" Lonto asked. "No bitch, Lieutenant. It's going to be a slow one, though. The people down there can go for weeks and not say crap within a block of a cop."

"You get the lab report yet?"

"I thought I'd stop before I went home," Lonto said. "Or did something come up?"

"You know Violet made detective this morning? I recommended him to the chief, and for once he said okay."

"He had the time in for promotion."

"I *know* he had the time in. I run this place. What I want to know is if he's a good cop out there on the street. You see him out there, I don't."

Lonto grinned slightly. "He's too good to waste on the fairy killer detail like you started me."

"Made you appreciate homicide, didn't it?"

"I loved it. How about we get Violet, so we don't get too much of a good thing?"

Jaworski shook his head and then shuffled papers on his desk, grinning at Lonto because he'd asked about something he'd intended to do anyway.

Lonto walked over to where he could stare out at the street. He had been around Jaworski long enough to know it wasn't going to do any good to argue. The Lieutenant, no doubt, already had Violet assigned and wanted to rub it in.

That's what Frenchie Labiche had tried to do. He had tried to make cute jokes about a dead pimp whom the cops were so fond of they sent the Third Ward's finest after his killer. And Lonto had not been in the mood for jokes after questioning reluctant whores.

"You need help on this Mack thing?"

"There should be a team working the Strip," Lonto said. "You know that."

"I thought you liked to work alone?"

"I do. I do because we're short. And because we're short, I've got a backlog of beefs laying on my desk that should go to robbery and burglary. But we know that a homicide dick is really just a jack-of-all-trades with a title that gets him the homicides because he's got experience. So, I do like to work alone, but right now I'd like to catch up some."

"I don't think Third Grade detectives should get on murders. He should start out easy."

"Horseshit!" Lonto said with conviction. "He's as broken in as he's going to get. He pounded a beat, and he rode prowl car. Now if he's going to be a dick, he can get down and root in the gutter with the rest of us. He don't need any more breaking in. He knows what dead people look like. And, Lieutenant, I would like to see the Doc; so if you just wanted my opinion on Violet, you got it. Can I get on with it?"

"Yeah," Jaworski said. "And take Violet with you. I don't want to hear a full-grown man cry about overwork around my station."

Lonto went to the door shaking his head. "Have you told him yet?"

"I told him." Jaworski smiled. "He's waiting in your office."

There was waiting being done on the Strip, too. Waiting that would likely see to it that the Third Ward bulls did not get too bored with their jobs. The pimps were waiting for the tricks to show so they could send them to their whores. Junkies were waiting for the pushers, who waited for delivery men. Jack-rollers were waiting for jacks to get drunk enough to be safe to roll, and derelicts just waited. It was a way of life.

A way of life that had got a shot in the arm when the army base outside the city had reopened. Soldiers did not help at all, and soldiers who were going to war made things as bad as those who were returning. It seemed that before they went there were two things on their minds: a good drunk, and a last piece of stateside ass to tide them over. And coming back, they changed the order of the two, having learned somewhere along the line that the drunk was best after they had sampled some stateside ass and retreated with their wallets still in their pockets. Retreated, before the whore's pimp could consider them drunk enough to put on his mugging coat with the lead pipe in its pocket.

Coming and going, the whores did a fast turnover, because the kid from End of Track, Nebraska, or such, was going to screw one honest-to-god whore before he went off to make Asia safe for American hamburger stands. And, too, he was likely to come looking for the same whore to celebrate his safe return before going back to End of Track.

There was a lot of money being spent between these comings and goings. But money drew more whores, and pimps, and muggers, and Lonto was of the opinion that the Strip already had its fair share, though he saw the value of a good roll in the hay for a war-bound boy. He wished they would find their roll somewhere else, and maybe he could come close to catching up on his own. Even if he had to marry her, which he was perfectly willing to do.

SIX

It was 10:00 p.m. when Cecil sat at the window of the unlighted room. Dora had long ago traveled to her pimp, leaving Cecil to dress slowly. He had pulled on one of the two pairs of civilian slacks he owned and a dark sports shirt. A lightweight windbreaker lay on the bed. It, too, was chosen for its dark color. His clothes fitted the night, he decided. And he took the knife from his bag and slid it into the chest sheath he wore under the shirt, before he went to sit at the window and watch the night grow.

In a place like the Strip death rides a lot of strange horses. It was a place where cruelty of man to man was a matter of fact. But usually each kick in the groin and stab in the back could be traced to a motivation, like an extra dime for a bottle of wine or a wife saying "Oh, Hans" when she should have been saying "Oh, José." Each a valid reason to bring death around in the mind of the dealer.

For Cecil, his reasons were valid. One, he liked it, and two, the world would be better off without pimps. They had robbed him of his first love. True, he had found a more lasting love in the knife, but the pimp had not known that when he'd put the girl on the street. In his mind there was the fact that murder wasn't really murder as long as there was a rational reason for it. It was perfectly all right to kill under certain circumstances; it was expected. All one needed was a reason. Liking it was not enough. So Cecil thought about his reasons.

He had been nineteen, and brave like a rock outside because he was going to war when he met her. His life, up until then, had been an almost total zero, with the one bright spot in it being the night he had lured a stray dog into the woodshed on his uncle's pig farm in Iowa and beaten it to death.

He had been unable to find anything else to experiment with in the dark before he had joined the Army to get away from the pig farm. And he was still wondering what it was all about when he spent his last three-day pass on the Strip, eager to get laid before he went to war.

He let on he knew all about it. He lied about it as seriously as the rest of them did. He even said he had laid Battalion Betty, the whore who waited outside the camp gate each night and took on all comers, regardless of race, creed, or color. So, with all the verbal experience, he'd been looking for a whore when he found Tillie.

It had been a hot day, and his uniform was sweat-soaked when he marched along Pimps' Row. At the corner of Sixth, he stopped to stare hungrily at the long legs Tillie was showing to him from the apartment building steps. She was showing him dark skin and brown hair to the best of her ability. She was wearing a white peasant blouse and white shorts, along with her best come-on look.

Cecil remembered exactly how she had been dressed. He remembered how good the rest of his pass had been. It had been so good that he left her with two months' pay and got on the troopship broke, with her address in his pocket.

If Cecil had known that he was the fourteenth soldier to believe in Tillie, he might have come back to the city to kill whores. Tillie at eighteen had a better system than Battalion Betty. Tillie was a whore with an angel's face and a virgin act that melted soldiers' hearts like piss through a snow bank.

Only Cecil didn't know, so he continued to think occasionally of his first love, and generally make an ass out of himself while he found his second love in the knife.

And these unknown facts were not the only probe that the fickle finger of fate had given Cecil. Tillie, as well as being a very smart young whore, had a monkey on her back as big as the world. She was a junkie. She shot her snow into her legs where not one of her fourteen-man task-force could have noticed, having other things on their minds when they might have. And also on her back, besides the monkey, was her high-class pimp, who had thought up the whole operation. Including the writing

51

of fourteen letters each week with which Tillie managed to wheedle pennies from heaven in the form of unspent combat pay her many lovers were getting.

Unfortunately, Cecil did not know these things. He did not know that the night Tillie had used a silk stocking to hang herself was the result of being out of heroin, money, and being told by her pimp that the sweet virgin act was over, worn out, and she was now among the curb-service whores. Tillie hanged herself because of these small problems, and not over the earth-shaking problem that Cecil was returning and would find her selling the promised land to all homesteaders. A problem that she would have solved with a mere "go get screwed" to Cecil's inquiring voice. That is, if she had been able to solve her other problems.

In all fairness to Tillie, it is safe to say that Cecil would have found another motive for which to enjoy killing. He might have taken a dislike to milkmen, or cab drivers, or even cops. But he didn't. He had a dislike for pimps, because not even his present whore had told him the truth about Tillie.

The fickle finger probed. Cecil lost his girl, and a pimp died. It was all very simple to Cecil. He would kill pimps and enjoy it until he found the one who had murdered Tillie. There were a lot of pimps. He put on his jacket with the pistol in its pocket and went out to find one.

Pepe Sanchez was the pimp he wanted to find. Cecil did not know Pepe. It was only that Cecil's current whore had fingered Pepe as her pimp. It was enough.

It was too goddamn much, Pepe was thinking over his third beer down at Frenchie's Bar. It was, indeed, too goddamn much. Too much for Pepe Sanchez, public provider of that warm-brown warmness that the Americans pay good dollars for to change their luck. It was very well to be a procurer for two such girls who treated him as the *jefe* of the business was properly treated. But the third one, Dora Valdez, was indeed too much.

Pepe began to spin his glass in slow, wet circles before him. Ai! It was when the girls had been born into the American cities that they did not make good wives or whores. Had Dora Valdez been raised in the city of Juárez, as the other two, she would be a good whore. But Dora had been raised in this monstrous American city where she learned no respect for her man.

Face it, Pepe, he told himself. Soon the other two will be telling you not to hand them that greaser dogshit, as Dora did, when you asked to be told who the man was in her room. That room was another matter. She should certainly be with the other two where one could properly watch them all.

He sighed heavily, feeling sorry for himself. He, Pepe Sanchez, would soon be treated as a common pimp by his own sisters because Dora Valdez did not have proper respect. After all that he had done for them, too. Of course, it was expected that one do what he could for his own blood.

Had he not seen to it that they did not become trapped in the whorehouses of Juárez? Had he not taken care that they were checked by the medico at the proper times? And it cost many dollars to arrange the papers so that they might come with him to the city, where they could become American citizens. What more could a brother do?

Pepe sipped his beer. It was perhaps a mistake to bring them here. They were much easier to handle when they were barefoot and hungry. In two years only they began to act like the American whores. The city and Dora Valdez would ruin his sisters.

But the city was good. There was money for the good clothes, and they were not strangers, in the way he had expected, for all along the Strip the people were strangers. There were Italians, and Polish, and the Jew men. And the dark Puerto Ricans that lived next to the Mexican blocks, where it was almost like Juárez on some nights. All were strangers to each other and accepted Pepe and his sisters with the same uncaring attitude that they had for each other.

Pepe was grateful for the city that had given him more money and finer clothes. If only it were not for Dora Valdez, who made some of the money but would teach the others American habits with her scorpion speaking. He could not understand why he had allowed himself to become the procurer for such a one. She would turn his very blood against him. A wonder that she had not already done so after an entire year. It was a sad thing that he must discipline Dora. It was better to keep the girls happy, but this must be done. It was the procurer's duty to do this, just as it was his duty to protect the girls from those bastard pimps who said it was not right that he, Pepe, procure for his own sisters, and tried to lure them away so that they might pimp for them. Pepe performed his duties.

Pepe had a six-inch dago switchblade in his pocket that the Jew next door had sold him. It was a fine knife, Pepe thought. He had never had so fine a knife to carry in the pocket of the good clothes in Juárez.

It was that fine knife, and his deft use of it, that kept Pepe in business on the Strip. His boyhood training in the art of gut-ripping in Juárez served Pepe well. Nobody was sure just where that wetback son-of-a-bitch, Sanchez, had learned to use a switchblade, but all the would-be takeover boys on the Strip were sure that he was one bad Mex to be screwing with. He looked it, too.

Pepe Sanchez was one of those people who seemed to have been ravaged by nature. He had a pointed head to start with, and hair that, while it was thick and black, grew in one direction from the top of his head, down, like an oiled haystack. Pepe had found that even the great American city did not have a barber who could do more than bowl-cut such hair. At times, Pepe wished he was in Juárez, where it was proper to wear the tall hat that would hide the difficult hair.

He wore American sunglasses to hide nature's prank with his eyes, for they were set close together though there was ample room for them to have been better spaced in his wide face. The eyes gave the appearance of studying closely the sides of his jutting nose, that, like his high cheekbones, spoke of Indian blood.

The cheeks also spoke of a long siege with smallpox, with their garnish of matchhead-size craters pitting the skin. Nature had given Pepe fine white teeth, and cheated him, too, because they made his weak chin seem weaker above the knobby Adam's apple on his thin neck.

The rest of Pepe's five-foot, eight-inch frame had matured with a diet of pinto beans, and tortillas when he was lucky. Pepe was as thin, and whipcord tough, as his ugliness called for—a fact that also helped to keep him in business. Pepe liked his business. He would, one day, be a great procurer like Frenchie Labiche, who owned a fine establishment like the bar he was in, and had girls of such beauty that men called on the phone for arrangements, and neither Frenchie nor the girls were forced to seek trade on Silver Street as Pepe was.

It would be good to be such a procurer, Pepe thought. But first one must have more girls, to make more dollars, even when it meant girls such as Dora Valdez. He must discipline Dora tonight, he decided. He would cut her only slightly, no more than he would his own sisters, only enough to make her learn that she must not allow a man to sleep with her unless it was for dollars.

Pepe finished his beer and held it up for Frenchie to see. A man must not work too hard, he thought. With the two sisters working at the present time, there remained only Dora to arrange for, to make it a nine-customer night.

Frenchie drew a glass of beer and placed it in front of him, nodding to a young man in one of the rear booths. "Boy back there wants you, Pepe."

Frenchie picked up a quarter while Pepe stared across the room.

"Wants to try some of that foreign stuff, I guess," Frenchie said. "Me, I like the U.S. grade, more class."

Pepe smiled and slid off the stool. The man in the booth was pale. Pepe had seen many pale ones from the soldiers' camp.

The man was looking down at his whisky glass when Pepe stopped at his booth. "You wanted to speak with me?" Pepe asked.

"Pepe Sanchez?" Cecil asked politely, and moved over to make room when he nodded.

The beat bull found Pepe bleeding to death behind a billboard in an empty lot on Sixth Street an hour later. It took the desk sergeant exactly four minutes to awake

Lieutenant Jaworski after he took the call. And it took Jaworski two minutes to tell Lonto to get his disciple Violet and go over to General to talk to a Mexican before he died. There was not any doubt that Pepe was in the process of doing just that. When he did, it would be homicide. So Lonto and Violet might get a jump on the case by being there before it became one for them. What the hell did they need sleep for, anyway?

Lonto was used to it, even two nights in a row. He knew that when he became a cop he became heir to the most screwed-up work schedule in the city. He had adjusted his sleep time accordingly. But he had never been able to adjust the mayhem so it would not interfere with his crash program of the seduction of Anna Ryan.

It was, in a way, fortunate that the mayhem came two nights in a row. The odds now favored that there would be peace for both the Strip and Lonto on the third night. Slaughter for three nights running would be an exception even for the Strip. And Lonto had a date with Anna Ryan that third night. Which was the rationalizing Lonto did for himself while he went out into the dark to check a homicide that wasn't a homicide yet.

Lonto didn't like any of it. There were suddenly too many corpses. A broken head, punched-in teeth, maybe a rape, and a certain amount of blood due to fist fights were expected each night on the Strip, but it had been quite a while since bodies had started to turn up in assembly-line fashion.

Violet was in the long hall on the second floor of General. He was making notes hurriedly because the beat bull that had brought Pepe in was in a hurry to get back to his partner who was pounding both their beats alone, and God knows the Strip was no place to cover two beats. He was in a hurry, but he listened patiently to everything the new detective asked him. He was saying, "There isn't a doubt it was a knife fight."

"You saw them fighting?" Violet asked.

"I didn't need to. This Sanchez lives on my beat. I know he's got a rep as a bad boy with a knife. So, when he turns up looking like he's been sliding on razor blades, and he's still got his switchblade in his hand, I don't need to be a detective to figure out that he wasn't cleaning his toenails back there."

"You found him about one-thirty, that right?"

"Yeah, I wouldn't have found him at all if I hadn't heard him praying back there. That lot's dark as hell, you know."

"Praying?"

The beat bull blinked. "With his switchblade still in his hand, he's flat on his back saying prayers to whatever saint he had. I don't understand Mex too well. But he was praying, all right."

"It was a good time to be doing it," Violet said. "Yes, sir, just in case you been riding the wrong horse all your life."

The beat bull patted his nightstick into his hand. "I put the flash on him and blew the whistle when I saw the mess. Had to ride the meat wagon over myself, because he looked like he wasn't going to make it and was maybe trying to spill something besides blood."

"Did he?"

"The Mex son-of-a-bitch spit in my face the one time he opened his eyes. Anyway, I wish they'd let the ambulance boys take dying statements, or put on some cops just riding the slaughter beefs."

"Did you notice anybody around?"

"She's a quiet beat that time of night," the bull said. "Tonight was no different. We don't get much on Sixth until after the bars close."

"It wasn't quiet tonight," Violet said. "By the looks of him, it was one hell of a fight."

"Like I said, he was a bad boy with a knife."

"Not bad enough. He's the only one in there dying, isn't he?" Violet asked.

The beat bull didn't try to answer.

SEVEN

IT WAS THURSDAY afternoon, and Violet was checking the whores of the newly expired Pepe Sanchez. Which left Lonto to check a few hundred other things that needed checking because there were now two dead pimps in the morgue, both of whom carried some very professional knifework. It was a situation that gave Lonto a mental pain in the ass, like Jaworski's.

The coroner had reported that Willie Mack had died from one knife wound in the back. That was not the way the coroner said it, but it was the way Lonto translated it. The wound was made by a double-edged instrument. The approximate length of the instrument was seven inches, a length that was very nicely suited to reach the heart and lungs from a low entry point.

This was not an unusual murder weapon, though the coroner also said that the murder weapon had a thicker blade than the usual switchblade, and was at least one inch wide at its widest point. Lonto would consider a hunting knife, rather than thin household cutlery, as a possible pimp sticker. Lonto knew quite a bit about the styles of gut rippers that were considered accessories to the well-dressed punk in the fashion eye of the Strip. It was not the knife that bothered Lonto as much as the fact that the same type of instrument had been used to bring about Pepe's death. And Pepe's own knife, which had been to the lab, did not have a trace of blood on its five-inch blade. Pepe had cut nothing but air with it.

Lonto was sure that Pepe had been trying to cut someone with it. Someone had certainly cut hell out of Pepe, and Lonto was thinking that Pepe would have been doing his best when it happened. At least until he had started to run out of blood, and, according to the way that the blood had stained Pepe's clothes, he had been on his feet during most of the bleeding.

There were other odd happenings that puzzled Lonto. Like both deaths being a result of a knife, thrust into the same area of the chest. Yet Pepe had three additional injuries, two knife slashes and a dislocated kneecap, each being a disabling wound. It was all so nicely done that Lonto was sadly impressed by their placement. Pepe had not been killed by a Silver Street punk, it seemed. He had been done in by an expert. So, why would an expert do in a pimp? It was a good question. Why would an expert do in two pimps? Lonto was going to need some luck to get answers in a place like Frenchie's Bar, where he had received no answers yesterday. Both dead men had used Frenchie's Bar as a favorite pimping post, one reason being that every man who hit the Strip with money in his pocket and an oil change on his mind visited Frenchie's. It was a local dive with an international reputation, a reputation that soldiers were inclined to spread when they remembered it as the last dive they'd been in before they shipped out. Soldiers, like cops, remember the worst best.

And Frenchie's was the worst in the eyes of the cops, a thorn they had never been able to quite pull out. It had been originally built as a bar to cater to the river trade. This type of architecture demanded that it have a large room for drinking, and several smaller rooms upstairs for the barge hands to practice whatever activity they had in mind at the moment.

Since that time the building had passed into the ownership of several men, including a Lopez, an O'Brien, a Cohen, and a Minelli, as well as some men who answered to titles like Graveyard Jones and Sleep-Out Willie. The bar was named, and renamed, according to the owner's choice, but it remained always as it was built, a bar with rooms upstairs, and a thorn to the cops. Under the ownership of Frenchie Labiche it remained a bar that catered to anyone who came in through its doors with the price of a drink, and kept the same policy of open trade for dope, free-lance whores, and pimps. Only the rooms upstairs changed. Frenchie didn't keep whores there. It was too risky, and he had a better arrangement for that. Instead, he filled the rooms with army surplus cots, separated them with chicken wire partitions, and rented a flop at four bits a night with a dirty blanket thrown in for another dime. Frenchie Labiche was not one to pass up a way to make a buck.

He'd made a buck or two in the slums of cities from Hong Kong to Pig Alley, and on to Beacon Street. Labiche was a heavy man with wide shoulders, a bullfighter's quickness, and a face that was the kind you forget. It was just a face, dark, with black eyes, and expressionless as an unused mirror. He had the charm of a hungry snake, and the temper of a castrated Mau Mau on a rape raid, but he was much too wise in the ways of the world to let his temper get him into something that he could not get his hide safely out of. He'd pimped, and thieved, and killed once or twice making a buck. And he was still making a buck at his bar with the same outlook on life. You make it any way you can.

So when Lonto came into the bar he did not expect a great deal of cooperation with the pimp killer problem. People like Frenchie didn't cooperate with cops unless they were questioned properly. And according to certain laws dealing with the questioning procedure, Lonto could not question Frenchie in the manner he would understand. He had to do the best he could, without beating hell out of Frenchie just to get the right time of day. Which is about the only way a cop could get it from Frenchie.

"Pepe Sanchez in here last night?" Lonto asked.

"I thought the Third Ward's finest got all the screwing they needed without a pimp's help," Frenchie said.

Lonto lit a cigarette and stared at the drunk down the bar, and then back at Frenchie. "Let's not go through that two days in a row," he said. "Try that one again. Was Pepe Sanchez in here last night?"

"Wasn't my day to watch him," Frenchie grinned. "I got better things to do than keep track of Mex pimps."

"How'd you like a visit from the Health Department, you son-of-a-bitch?" Lonto asked seriously. "Some new boys that won't take?"

"I don't have to take that . . ."

"You're going to take the same kind of shit you hand out. I'm fed clear up to the ass with your crap. I'll make life so goddamn miserable for you that you'll think the station house is home. I got lots of time, now how about it?"

"I'm scared to death."

"I knew you'd be," Lonto said. "That's what I want to talk about, death."

Frenchie smiled and poured himself a drink, watching Lonto over the bar. "Sure, because everybody fingers my place. You visit any of the other bars?"

"Not yet," Lonto said. "If he worked out of some of the others, I'll get to them. Right now, I'm here."

"You lived down here, cop. You know how it is. We keep the pimps out, and they take the customers to some other bar. You got to give a little, you know."

"I know how it is," Lonto said. "Was he in here last night?"

"Sure, but I didn't see him leave with anyone. I don't want to be watching line-ups just because he was in here."

"What time?"

"Like I told you, I wasn't watching him."

Lonto was silent, watching *him*.

"Could have been around eleven—twelve, maybe. Last time he came to the bar. He's a nurser, you know; sits all night over a couple of beers."

"But you didn't see him leave with anyone? Talk to anyone?"

"I'm busy back here," Frenchie said. "I'll give it to you straight, cop. I can't see anything. I blab what I see, and I got no business. Hell, who's going to say they seen this guy? He shivved two cats already, didn't he?"

"Did he?"

"Don't give me that routine," Frenchie said. "You got ears. I ain't seen a pimp out all day. Who knows who's next?"

Lonto smiled. "I hear you're still running some call girls, Frenchie. Suppose this guy does have a thing for pimps, and decided on you next? I'll bet you could remember a few things then."

"Hey! Wait a minute!" Frenchie said. "You ever seen me pimp in here? You ever see a whore call me boss?"

"No." Lonto grinned happily. "But then we wouldn't, when you work by phone. You be real careful, Frenchie. One of these days you're going to send one of your girls to a vice cop."

"Crap! You ain't got a thing on me there."

Lonto sighed and slid off the stool. "I kid you not, Frenchie. Everybody on the Strip knows you're a pimp—uptown grade, but still a pimp. If you're right about this guy it might be a good idea to stir up your memory some. You could be third man on the list."

"Crap," Frenchie said again, and watched Lonto's retreating back until he reached the door. "I'll let you know if I remember anything, cop."

"You might," Lonto said. "You just might, now."

Frenchie stopped smiling and finished his drink. He shivered some when the cop was gone. The bastard was closer to right than he knew. He had been worried about getting rubbed before, plenty of times. But it was one thing to know who's doing the rubbing, and a very different thing when someone started pulling names out of a hat, and killing just because they were pimps. So what's wrong with being a pimp? Man, it's getting so a man can't make a buck at all. All the time cops, and now this creep comes along.

Frenchie mixed another drink and sipped at it. He set the glass on the bar and stared at the back booth, where Pepe had done his last business the evening before.

What did that creep look like? A wiry bastard, like that dago cop, only sort of girlish-looking. And pale, like he'd been in a dark place too long. Can't remember that face, though. The cat hadn't looked like he'd be able to pull a sick whore off a piss pot. Sure fooled hell out of Pepe.

He ran a thick hand over his shirt and scratched an armpit, jerked his head at the extra bartender, and walked back to his office. The dago cop had stirred that place in Frenchie that helped him stay alive in nearly every variety of trouble. The same place that made him cut or shoot or pound first, when there was the slimmest chance of his being treated in a similar manner.

And the problem rested on the thin edge of chance. Was there *any* possibility that his name was on the pimp killer's list? That's what they were calling him, the Pimp Killer, and the pimps were believing in him after last night. That girlish-looking cat had put the fear in them all right. But that was their problem. Or was it?

He put his feet up on his desk, and watched the sweat beading the glass in his hand. This pimp killer business gave you the willies; made you think. Funny thing how fear spreads. Two pimps dead, and, right away, every pimp around is running scared. They won't help the cops, but they get nervous. Like he was nervous. He knew he was going to be careful about who he dealt with. There was too much money around to slow down with the girls. And he had enough steady, important men as customers to lose a lot of dollars if he slowed down. Too damn much to lay aside if he wanted to be careful, or was scared. Hell, he wasn't scared.

He just had to be careful. The cops will pick the creep up, and if he killed a few more pimps before they did, it would just help business. All there was to do was be careful.

But, baby, if I see your girlish puss on the streets or in my bar again, I'll feed you a mickey and drown you in the slop bucket before I dump you into the river. It would be my one and only favor to the cops.

He opened the desk drawer and glanced through the address book he kept there. Six dates for tonight. Three hundred easy bucks, tax-free bucks. Too bad you had to take a fifty-fifty cut with these classy bitches. They should all be like them Jap dolls—a few yen, or a slap in the head. There wasn't any of those kind in the States. God-damn States even turned pimping into an enterprise. They should have a union. Call Girls Incorporated, or some such shit.

Like that Mex bitch, half-Mex, anyway. Talk about getting high hat. What the hell did I tell her? Put a mattress on your back and start a curb service, Tillie. Man, and what's she do? Goes home and hangs herself, that's what she does. Oh, they're sensitive bitches when you teach them some class, and show them how to work a trick. That stupid ass Tillie could have been still making

a buck if she hadn't let the dope start screwing her up
Started to look like a dog, too. Well, tough shit, Tillie
Can't use junkies for uptown, so it's just as well you
topped out. That had been good young ass, though
Probably had them soldier boys thinking they had got a
cherry. They sure get to thinking fancy when they make
more than five bucks a lay, though.

This last one was getting that way, too. And what the
hell had she been when she came here? A round-heeled
floozy. All you get nowadays is floozies. Cat house or
pick-up bait, with no class, and I got to start with that
because I need fifteen girls that can work it worth a hun
dred bucks. I got the best trade in town, and no rough
stuff. I made this dive international, like they call it. Al
the army brass, hot-shot businessmen—this is where they
call. I send them a lady. And all I get to work with is
floozies! Garbage!

What'd this last bitch say? I've been thinking of quit
ting, Frenchie? Yeah, that's what she said. Simple bitch
She came here willing to screw the first drunk she found
for a fin, and I got her working it four times a week for
two hundred bucks and living uptown.

Frenchie slammed the glass down, and shoved the ad
dress book into his pocket. Okay, Miss High and Mighty
Ryan. After I get back the money for the time I wasted
on you I'll kick your ass out on the street.

After I get my money back. Frenchie wrote a client's
address down, and looked at the phone. Better have a
talk with the bitch. She's got that quitting idea. I'll keep
her ass so busy she'll get blisters on it.

He smiled to himself. She'd like that. She was the kind
that likes it fast and often. Like they're trying to screw

he world. First she can't get enough, and now she wants
o quit?

Frenchie put on his jacket, and went out through the
ar. "Take the calls, will you, Jack? I'll be back in an hour
r so."

The bartender smiled at him with slack lips. "Sure,
oss," he said. "You're going out, huh?"

"No, you stupid son-of-a-bitch," Frenchie said, "I'm
oing to stand outside and watch you steal from the till."

"I ain't stealing, boss."

Frenchie went on out. Idiots and floozies, he thought.
diots, floozies, and now this creep with the knife run-
ing around. It's a wonder a guy can make a buck at all.

He unlocked his car, and slid in behind the wheel,
atching Trashcan O'Toole unwrapping papers on the
orner. You can bet they're full of this creep. The Pimp
iller! Huh! Bunch of shit!

Frenchie said it, but he didn't believe it deep down in
is guts. There was a cold little knot of fear growing
ere.

He scrubbed sweat from his face and brought the car
o life, squealing into the street. Maybe the son-of-a-bitch
id kill pimps—screw him.

It was a good idea to take Anna Ryan the name of her
ick for tonight. She was a hot little number. As torrid
s any he'd laid. She must really pussy-whip them old
astards.

So, it was a good idea to straighten her out about the
uitting crap and get some of the nervousness worked
ut of him. It would be a mistake to let some bastard
ng-dick him out of that little money-maker. That little
oney-maker was going to get the Labiche easy treat-

ment first. Make it so good she won't be so anxious t
get away. It would keep her from thinking she migl
like a steady hump.

Frenchie spat out the window. Could be she alread
had a steady hump. Can't keep track of all the floozie
but Anna was going to get some attention. Sure get son
damn fool notions, these floozies. They start thinkin
they're people after a while. Like that dago punk wh
thinks he's God 'cause they gave him a badge.

Well, someone will show him he's not. Maybe th
creep. I'd sure like to see this creep stick a shiv into th
cop's guts. Hell, maybe he will.

Frenchie wiped sweat from his face and smiled. Yea
maybe he will.

EIGHT

ED VIOLET had questioned few whores before. And never two dark-haired sisters whose English was not very good. And his Spanish was terrible. Violet had twelve years on the force before they took away his uniform and put him into a detective's suit. He found that he had not yet reached the point where nothing surprised him.

Pepe Sanchez being a pimp for his sisters surprised him, and realizing that he had put them on the street at the tender age of twelve in Mexico, where it is hard to be a whore at any age, *really* surprised him. But what topped it all off was that they'd grieve his loss. Pepe's other whore couldn't have cared less that Pepe was dead,

71

and said so. Which was about all Violet had got from her besides a cup of coffee.

And all that the sisters had given him was what a fine, brave man their brother was. That and a bewildered view of a dead pimp were all Violet had to show for his first day's work as a detective.

He had no illusions about being a cop. He was a cop because his father had been a cop, and his father's father had been a cop. There were a hundred things that he'd rather be than a cop. Like an eight-to-five lunch-bucket carrier who came home nights, put the kids to bed, patted his wife on the rump, and sat down to watch TV or bitch about the bills. He was a cop because it was expected of him. There had never been any question about what he would be. Now that he was, he was trapped. It was as simple as that.

Papa had crawled around in the slime. So I finally get to crawl around in slime, Violet thought. Life is a big trap for guys like me. You get caught, and you got a wife and kids to see that you stay caught. Boxed in with the hope of a pension that I'm hooked to with the years of being a cop. Who wants to be a detective cop, for Christ's sake? It's bad enough being a beat cop in a nice quiet residential district, or being on prowl car. That's all the advancement I want, prowl car. Nice and easy there, or a desk job. But what's Jaworski do? He says, Ed, you got to move up. Who ever heard of a cop who don't want a promotion?

Violet had heard of one. What was a promotion, anyway? More work and a new title. It didn't make sense. With his years, he drew nearly as much pay as a dick, without the headaches. Aw, the hell with it.

In the trap everything stinks, like this case. I got no

stomach for this. Lonto, now, he can see this slime and be a cop in it. Me, I'd just as soon ignore it until someone else cleans it up. Well, this is where you start helping with the cleaning, Ed boy. Now you get to be the cop Papa wanted you to be. And the nagging fear came back that being a so-so cop for twelve years hadn't been smart. Doing just enough to get by.

Papa had helped there, too, he realized. Getting him an easy beat to start with. No hard stuff in residential. And just enough to make a man jumpy on prowl car. So he'd been promoted to detective a little later than family tradition called for, but he'd got there without wading in the dregs—or having to point a pistol at a man. Now it wasn't going to be that way. On the Strip a cop wound up shooting to do his job, sometimes to save his own life. Either way, he didn't know if he could.

Hell of a thing if they found out that the thought of shooting a man made him sick. Ruin everything. Even a son-of-a-bitch like Sanchez, who made his own sisters into whores, was human. He crossed his mental fingers. There was Lonto. There was always the chance that Lonto would be close when there was heavy stuff. A chance that would let him continue the farce of being a cop's cop like Papa. That was the way he'd have to play it in the trap that he had nothing to do with choosing.

He looked back at the apartment building where Pepe Sanchez had kept two of his whores, and then at his watch. He decided that his first day in the slime with his new detective suit had been as miserable as he had expected it to be.

For Anna Ryan, the night would be miserable, too, if the visit from Frenchie was any indication of what was

73

to come. She gave him a practiced smile at the door, and her mind was already searching for a reason, other than the usual, with which she could make herself unavailable for the night. Maybe a lot of undependability would get her free of him and let her work something out with Tony Lonto. If she was any judge of men, Tony was anxious enough for her, so he'd accept the fact that she was a call girl.

Frenchie pushed inside the apartment, reaching out to pinch her breast as he did so. "Honey, I can see why you're popular," he said. "I came all the way over here just to be sure I'm right, and to tell you who your trick is for tonight."

"You could have phoned."

"You can't get samples over the phone," Frenchie said. "You wouldn't be wanting to back off our deal or something, would you? Fifty-fifty and samples, remember?"

Anna shrugged. She gave Frenchie an oblique look, back over her shoulder. She saw that he was following her into the bedroom. Watching his eyes, she decided that it was a bad time to beg off. His eyes were flatly cold, but maybe that would change after she took him to bed. She'd made the choice often before; there was a softness in men after. Even a pimp could be bent further. And maybe he'd let her off for the night then.

His eyes were still cold when Anna turned to face him from beside the bed and began unbuttoning her blouse. "Last few times," she said, "you didn't seem interested in samples."

"I'm interested now," he said. "I like it better when it might not be around much longer."

She draped her blouse over the foot of the bed, and

74

stood facing him with a smile. "Get as much as you can, Frenchie. I'm still thinking about quitting."

"When?"

"Not before you get some," she answered. "But I'm just thinking. You know I'll tell you when."

He took off his jacket and studied her. "I like them high tits. Like a Jap's—hard and high, only bigger."

"Thanks," she said. "They pay enough for them." She slipped out of her skirt and panties and lay on the bed. "I thought you were so hot for this?"

"We got time," he said. "I don't want you quitting for a few months yet."

She stared at him. "I could have just left town, you know. I'm sticking with our arrangement."

"Be sure you do," Frenchie said, walking to the bed. "You still got a few tricks to do before I break even. Got that? You're going to stay until I make . . . say, another thousand on you."

"That's almost three months." Anna frowned, watching him undress. "I don't know . . ."

He sat on the bed and rubbed her breast. "Sure you know," he said. "You like it too much to quit. I know you do."

She was silent for several minutes, feeling his hands kindle the fire in her. "You know too damn much."

"Like what you need." He smiled and kissed her breast. "Like I know what you're looking for. . . . Like that?"

She shivered. "I don't do it like . . . Yes, don't stop."

He was necessarily silent for several moments.

"Yes," Anna said again. "Don't stop."

He did, and smiled at her. "It gets better," he said, watching her shift up on the bed. "Thought you'd go for this; little dyke in you, I think. Never tried it?"

"No," she said. "Hurry."

"Sure," he said. "You won't want to quit then."

"All right," Anna whispered. "Show me why I won't . . . just . . . like . . . that . . ."

Frenchie showed her. He showed her the art of Labiche bed-fighting that had earned him the name of "that goddamn Labiche with the pistol grip ears" among his girls who had thought of quitting and stayed to experiment.

When Frenchie's whores decided to quit the second time, he simply beat the hell out of them to discourage such thoughts. But first he tried the Labiche special. Sometimes it worked.

On Anna Ryan it worked well enough to make her forget that she had wanted the night off. It didn't quench the fire in her as Lonto did, but it made Anna postpone quitting the trade to raise blond dago kids, at least for one night.

He'll appreciate it more if I make him wait, Anna thought, when she called Lonto and broke their date.

Lonto would have appreciated it any way he could have got it, but as it appeared that he wasn't going to, he appreciated the only thing he could. There didn't seem to be any mayhem on the Strip to pull him from bed on three nights in a row. Which is where he went, to dream blissful dreams about Anna Ryan and to wonder occasionally why anyone would want to kill pimps with precision.

Cecil knew exactly why he wanted to kill pimps. The trouble seemed to be that not everyone agreed with him. The pimps didn't agree, but that was to be expected and welcomed by Cecil. It certainly wouldn't be as satisfying to kill a pimp who wanted to be killed, would it? Now, Pepe Sanchez certainly hadn't wanted to die, and killing him had been much more enjoyable than killing Willie Mack had been.

At least Cecil thought so. He thought murder mixed with other enjoyable things—very well. Take sex now, that was much better when it was followed with a murder. There was no denying that, as he'd found out. And when you mix a good murder, sex, and the fear he'd enjoyed seeing in Pepe's eyes, it all added up to a very good reason for killing pimps. With fear in the pimps, and a woman after, it wasn't even necessary to have a good reason like revenge. Cecil hadn't remembered Tillie at all when he'd killed Pepe. But Tillie was a good thing to remember later. It gave him a reason to look for more pimps.

Now, if you had all these very good reasons, it would be hard to understand why people besides pimps didn't seem to agree with them, wouldn't it?

Like the newspapers. You'd think they'd have other things to print on the front page besides the killing of two pimps. Because printing it made people read it, and talk about it. And talking about it made pimps unwilling to admit that they were pimps. It could make it hard to find a pimp to kill if that's what you wanted to do. That's what the newspapers were doing when they printed crap like: KNIFE SLAYER STALKS CITY, and go on to make it perfectly obvious who was being stalked, and generally acting like they didn't approve.

But Cecil could find something to like in the news. The pimps would be very frightened when he found them. That should make the next one even better than Pepe.

Oh, Pepe had been very brave at first. Cecil lay on the bed in Dora's room and thought about Pepe. He remembered just how easy it had been. It had been foolish of Pepe to think he could fight an expert. But, then, Pepe hadn't known that until it was too late and he had a crippled leg to keep him there. There was one thing to say about war. It certainly made one an expert. Of course, it would have been better if it had lasted longer. Well, it had been good enough. The next one would be better, because there would be more fear in him. That was something to think of. How good would it be if there was some way to warn them it was coming?

Cecil smiled in the dark and thought about it. He could see that it might be dangerous because the police didn't agree, like the newspapers didn't. But they couldn't stop him. Maybe they could. But not until he found Tillie's pimp.

Just to be safe, Tillie's pimp was next. He'd be the best. They would understand his reasons better after that. They would understand why he enjoyed it after that. They couldn't help but agree with him when they knew, could they?

It did not really matter to Cecil if people agreed or not. It was very clear to him. Pimps needed killing, and it was logical that he kill them, because he had a reason and he liked it. It was just too bad that the police and the newspapers might make it hard to find another pimp.

Cecil's smile thinned when he heard the click of high heels pass in the hall. Dora might give him trouble, too. But would she? Jesus Christ, that had maybe been a mistake. It should have been another pimp besides hers. He could see that now. Especially since she knows how I hate the bastards. How much did she guess? Had she worked it out why I asked so many questions about Pepe? No, she couldn't have or she wouldn't have let Tillie's pimp's name slip. Labiche. Frenchie Labiche, that dirty bastard that steered me to Pepe last night. I had him right there and didn't know it.

That was bad, too. Frenchie knew what he looked like now. Maybe it was good. But did that goddamn Dora let it slip on purpose? Did she think I might spill something?

How much did she guess?

Cecil lit a cigarette and considered his conversation with Dora, after she had told him that her pimp was the second murder.

"You'd better spend tomorrow in a bar, honey," Dora had said.

"Why?"

"Cops. That stupid Pepe had two sisters working for him, and they both know where I live. There'll be cops here tomorrow."

"Why should I worry about them?"

Her eyes seemed to fasten on his face. "It's just better you're not around. Why get mixed up at all? You know how cops are."

He laughed shortly. "You think they might think I killed your pimp because of you? Why should I?"

She had undressed silently and slid into the bed with him. "That's how cops are, honey. And I'll have to go out tomorrow, anyway—today, I should say, it's three already."

He stared at her paleness in the dark. "I suppose you're going to look for another pimp?"

"Please, Cecil. I told you it's easier than walking the streets. Pepe wasn't much, but he was better than nothing."

He laughed and pulled her to him. "He was scum. Like Tillie's pimp. Maybe he'll take you on if you need one so bad."

"He won't," she whispered.

He couldn't stop the question that rose to his lips. "How do you know? You said you didn't know him."

She was quiet for a moment. "I was worried that you might get into trouble if you knew."

He felt the excitement building in him then. "So you lied for a pimp?"

"For you," she said. "He's a pretty nasty customer for a kid like you to pick on."

He pulled her hard against him. "Does that feel like a kid?" he demanded. "It doesn't matter who the bastard is. I told you I'm over that."

"Good," she whispered. "I'm afraid Labiche would have hurt you if you'd mentioned Tillie to him."

Cecil put the cigarette out in the ash tray beside the bed. That's how she'd told him, he thought. Just like that. Did it mean anything?

There was a thin feeling of fear in Cecil. It was not a fear of what would happen if he were caught. It was a fear that he would not be able to kill another pimp before he was.

He lay awake for a long time in the dark, thinking of ways to make the next one very good—better than Pepe, in case it was his last. And when he went to sleep he thought he had succeeded.

NINE

LEUTENANT JAWORSKI knew what he had when he faced Lonto and Violet across his desk on Friday morning. There were other things in the station that gave him a pain in the ass besides Lonto. He had two of them on his desk.

"Have you two read this?" he asked, tapping the newspapers with a thick finger. "In case you don't know it, they're full of this guy you're supposed to be interested in."

"Yes, sir," Violet said. "Quite a build-up, isn't it?"

Jaworski stared at Lonto thoughtfully. "What have we

got here, Lonto? A goddamn Jack the Ripper with a ne
twist?" He paused, and picked up a memo slip. "And th
is from the Commissioner. He wants to know what t
hell we're doing about this. I want to know what I shou
tell him. What have you two been doing?"

"Doing?" Lonto asked. "Let's see, yesterday there we
four burglar beefs and a robbery to check out. And the
were a couple of people to see about the ones from t
day before that. Not to mention these two homicides th
involve a few dozen whores who don't want cops aroun
That's what we were doing."

The Lieutenant was silent until Lonto grinned. "Oka
so you're busy. Now what have you got? Let's kick
around some."

"I think they're right," Lonto said. "The papers, I mea
This guy's out to kill pimps. Same guy, both cases. A p
with a knife."

"What do you mean?"

"You see the report on Sanchez? He was slashed in u
usual places before he took the one in the chest."

"Suppose he just walked into a better punk with
knife than he is?" Violet asked.

"A punk with a shiv don't fight like that," Lonto i
sisted. "A punk cuts any damn place he can cut. This g
cut Sanchez where there was a main artery close to t
surface. And where Sanchez didn't expect a man to try
cut him—high on the inside of the arms. A pro fights li
that, feints a thrust to the body, and cuts a limb arte
coming back." Lonto shook his head. "I asked Doc
check these; the cuts were made when the knife was co
ing away from Sanchez."

"A faked thrust, and a slash when he recovered," Viol
said. "Still could be a punk."

Jaworski watched Lonto and waited.

"Could be," Lonto said. "But the switchblade set don't carry a double-edged shiv. And you show me one that will judo-kick a man like Sanchez was. That knee is just too much coincidence for me to buy. Both chest wounds were right where they had to be, too. No misses, no glancing off bone. One shot, and right where it should go if you know your business. Same thing with Willie Mack."

"Still could be a coincidence," Violet argued. "Not connected . . ."

"All right. All right," Jaworski said. "Let's hear why."

"For one thing, Willie Mack was rolled," Violet said. "His wallet was missing. That could have been the reason for him."

Jaworski stared at Lonto. "Doesn't this guy know anything?" he asked. "Jesus Christ, Violet! The body was found on Pimps' Row! You can't blink down there without losing your wallet. It's lucky he still had his pants when we found him."

Lonto agreed. "We get a lot of it, Ed. A dead man is easier to roll than a drunk. The dead don't care, they figure."

"Have you got anything else to go on?" Jaworski asked. "Anything at all from the lab?"

"I'll bring it in," Lonto said. "It reads like a microscopic life history, including the fart stains in their shorts. Only one thing in it that's unusual."

"Go ahead," Jaworski said.

"There were traces of a cleaning compound in the knees of Willie Mack's trousers. Lab says it's the type of stuff they use to clean car upholstery. It's a locally made type called Kar Klean, spelled with K's instead of C's."

"Willie didn't own a car?"

"Willie didn't own anything, or hang around anythin that would be cleaned often enough to count."

"He was in a newly cleaned car, then," Jaworsksi said "How's that help us?"

"A new one, or a rented one, Lieutenant. I like th rented one, if he picked it up in the killer's car. It wa raining that night, so I think a rented one."

"You check this?"

"We're not triplets," Lonto said. "We can maybe get done today, this area at least. It'll be one hell of a jol all the rental cars that went out freshly cleaned."

"I'll get someone on it," Jaworski said. "Violet can ru down the ones that look good. Okay, I'll buy a singl man on both jobs. Same type weapon, same M.O. We g a Jack the Ripper with a new twist, then."

"What about him being a professional knife man? Violet demanded. "I can't see how you can be so sure."

"I'm not," Lonto grinned. "But we haven't got anythin else to go on. I recognize the place where he might hav learned his art."

"What do you mean?" Jaworski wanted to know.

"It's a bitch, Lieutenant," Lonto said. "I don't like th idea, but you don't go to a seminar to learn knife fightin; You don't learn it on the streets either, not this style."

"You're thinking that this guy is a soldier?" Jaworsl asked. He blinked at Violet.

"If it's the same guy," Violet said. "Tony should kno what they teach."

"Pretty slim," Jaworski growled. "There's a few thou sand guys coming and going through here every month

"It gets worse," Lonto smiled. "He could be a vet, an

84

om any branch that teaches knife work and judo in
mbat. Or I could be way off, and he learned it at finish-
g school."

"But you don't think so?"

"No," Lonto said. "I don't think so. I remember in our
tfit, only a few guys ever got good at that type of fight-
g. It's an art, judo and the knife. And when you're good,
u're one dangerous son-of-a-bitch to go up against. I
ink Sanchez found that out."

Jaworski leaned back in his chair. "This is all you have
work with?"

"That's it," Lonto said. "It's going to be one of them
ng ones, unless we get a break. Until we do, we guess."

Jaworski stared at the newspapers on his desk. "Then
t on it. I want this bastard in a cell before he gets the
ole city screaming," he said. "You know what the Com-
ssioner said? He said if we can't catch a nut that's
lling pimps, how can we be expected to protect honest
izens."

"Does it make any difference who's the homicide?"
nto asked.

"Figure of speech," Jaworski grinned. "Let's keep him
ppy."

Lonto studied him blandly. He knew the Lieutenant
s only telling him there was pressure on him. There
s always pressure when the newspapers played up an
usual crime. "We'll keep him happy," he said. "Tell
n that the psychoanalyst said he didn't have a thing to
rry about if he hasn't been pimping. This guy likes
mps."

"Get on it," Jaworski said, and tossed the newspapers
the wastebasket. He looked at Violet. "Don't jump to

conclusions, Violet. Make guesses, like him, but don't ̶ ̶
crap like that wallet make up your mind so you can't s ̶
it any other way."

Violet nodded and followed Lonto out. So people did ̶
rob the dead in residential, he thought. So I don't knc
how a pro killer uses a knife. I didn't want this. I do ̶
want to learn it. All I want is a nice quiet beat, whe ̶
people act like people. So, to hell with it.

And when Violet told himself to hell with it, in ̶
mind, he went to the phone to start a check on car ren ̶
agencies that might or might not have rented a car to ̶
killer. It was tiresome, routine work that made being
cop what it was. But it was also clean work. It was bet ̶
than talking to whores who had a dead brother for
pimp.

Let Lonto talk to the whores, Violet thought. He's us ̶
to it.

Lonto, at the time, was on his way to talk to a who ̶
but he didn't know it. It did not have a thing to do w ̶
his duties as a detective. Lonto wanted to see Anna Ry ̶
because he had not seen her last night or furthered ̶
seduction schedule one bit. It was going to be a bitch
a job talking Anna into raising blond dago kids when th ̶
both had working hours that interfered with their getti ̶
together. He condemned both jobs though he was ̶
sure yet just what Anna's was, except that she had brok ̶
a date to do some work for her boss. That was enough.

Jesus Christ! I'm in love! Lonto thought. How stu ̶
lucky can a guy get? I'll even like Jaworski. I'll inv ̶
him to the wedding. There's got to be a wedding. A ̶
need is some time with her. All right, so she hasn't me ̶
tioned marriage, but all I need is some time to take c ̶

86

of that. Not just a quick visit, like this morning will be.

What kind of life is that? Just a visit, because there's a killer loose. Got to explain that to her, too. I'm a cop, Anna. I'll always be a cop, and the best husband I can be in between times. It would only be fair to tell her that. Start it out right, level and honest. No other way to start.

Does this killer know all the trouble he's causing? The Commissioner's upset over you, mister, and you are fouling up my love life. You are also making new detective Violet wish that he was back on prowl car, because he's trying to tell himself that people like you don't exist. But we're going to show you to him. So, why don't you do something stupid and help us some? Give us all a break, and maybe I can find some time to get married, then.

I wish I knew why you kill pimps. I certainly wish that I did. I've seen a lot of nuts come out of the Strip, but you're the first one that the stoolies don't have anything on. Know what that means, mister? It means that you're a stranger around here, because everybody knows everyone's business on the Strip, and somebody is going to let it leak. But not with you. You are going to be tough to catch because of that. Until you make a mistake. I hope you made that mistake already. I'm going to check every soldier that was on pass those two nights. It's going to be one hell of a job, but I only have to check the overnight passes, which will cut it down some. Maybe it's a shot in the dark, like Violet thinks. But we're used to them. That maybe was your mistake, a pass, and knife training that you are so very good at, and maybe a rented car to go along with all that. One that we haven't found yet.

But you could do something stupid and save me all that trouble, because I could be wrong and I'll have to start somewhere else. I'll bet you have no idea all the trouble you're causing. I would love to be able to spend a whole hour with my girl, but I can't because of you. So do something stupid, mister. Like I did when I became a cop who can't find time to tell his girl that he loves her.

Hell, I think I'm afraid to do that.

Lonto glanced at his watch while he waited for the light to change. It was ten thirty-two.

At ten forty, Anna handed him a cup of coffee in the kitchen of her apartment. She touched his hand and smiled. "Mad about last night?"

Lonto grinned foolishly and shook his head. "Thinking about a case. Working hours, you know," he said. "I never get mad, it's one of my few virtues. Never get mad at a pretty woman. Even when they stand me up for their boss."

She made a face at him. "That's good to know. I'll take advantage of it when we're married. Are you working on the murders that are in the papers?"

Lonto was working on them in his mind, which was in the usual fogged state that it reached when he was with her. Between the case and the fog, he almost missed her words. He had the cup halfway to his mouth when he realized what she had said.

"Say that again."

"Are you working on these murders? The . . ."

"Not that," he told her. "Are you really going to take advantage of my virtues—when we're married?"

"Did I say that?" she asked. "I probably will, then."

He set his cup back down and grinned some more. "How about that?" he asked in amazement. "When can we get . . ."

"Don't," Anna told him. "Please wait a while, Tony. Then ask, and I'll say yes."

"How long?" he wanted to know. "Tomorrow, day after?"

"You'll know when," Anna said. "But let's wait, and see if you still want to then."

"I want to now," he said seriously. "And I'll still want to next week, or next month. I don't think I'll last much longer than that. I love you, Anna."

"I know," Anna smiled. "Waiting won't matter, then, will it, Tony?"

"Nothing will matter, Anna," he said, and sat there grinning.

"Your coffee's getting cold," Anna murmured. "The case again?"

"Hell, no. I'm in shock," Lonto said. "If I move, I'll wake up or something. Can I take you to dinner tonight?"

She frowned. "You're going to hate me," she said. "I've got to work again. That's why I'm off now." She moved around the table and kissed him. "You seemed angry last night, so I didn't tell you then. I wanted to see you, and we could plan this weekend."

"Saturday night, then," he said. "I guess we'll have to get used to odd hours. But they'll only come from *my* job after we're married."

Anna kissed him again, and slid into his lap. Saturday night would be fine. Her week's quota of tricks would be filled tonight.

"After you ask. Remember?" she said.

"I already have."

"You'll know when to ask again. Then I'll let you chain me to the kitchen stove."

Lonto shifted embarrassedly. "God, woman! It'll be to the bed, not the stove."

Anna kissed his ear. "You don't need a chain. Just you."

"Sure you can't get off tonight?" Lonto pleaded.

"Can you spare an hour now?" she teased, and wiggled in his lap.

Lonto rolled his eyes back in mock disgust. "You're bribing the law, lady. Lured me up here, and tried to seduce me when I can't. Sure you can't get off tonight?"

"I'll bribe you Saturday night, okay?"

Lonto sighed. "Then you'd better let me up so I can lock up every hood in town. I'm going to make sure that's one date I *don't* miss." He sobered. "Kitten, I've got to run. It's almost eleven, and I've got to see a man."

"Eight o'clock Saturday?" she asked.

"Try to keep me away," Lonto said. "This is one cop that knows a good thing when he sees it."

Trashcan O'Toole knew a good thing when he saw it, too. It was a ten-dollar bill which the man in front of his newsstand held.

"Sure," Trashcan said. "I know Labiche, but he ain't in his place yet. He don't get around till noon."

"I can't wait," the man said. "It's worth ten to me to see that he gets this note."

Trashcan took the envelope, and the bill. "I'll see he gets it, mister. Who should I say sent it?"

"Tell him I was in the other night," the man said. "He'll know who sent it." He grinned thinly. "Maybe he's expecting it."

"Yeah," Trashcan said. "I'll tell him. You new around here?"

The man picked up a newspaper and folded it under his arm. "I'm new all over," he said, and walked off.

"Wise ass," Trashcan muttered. "Didn't pay for the paper, either."

He considered the envelope in his hand. Who sends that bastard Labiche letters? he thought. Guy probably wants a doll for the night, and don't want to be seen in that dive. That's what it probably was. Trashcan wasn't about to open the envelope and find out. He *did* know a good thing when he saw it. The envelope looked like a good thing to keep his nose out of.

He shrugged, and sat down to bastardize some more poetry while he waited for Labiche to show.

He wrote:

> By the shores of Dank and Dirty,
> By the reeking, scum-filled water,
> Lies a street of man's creation,
> Dredges of man's evil building.
>
> New around it rose the city,
> Shining bright with man's new wonders;
> Far above it shines man's new thirst,
> Ancient stars of the universe.
>
> But on the street, the thirsts run small,
> Canned heat and aftershave for alcohol;
> Switchblades flicker on fate of a dime,
> Precious silver, the price of wine.
> Rape and plunder, thieve and kill,
> Dredges festering in a man-made hell.
>
> This the street of man's creation,
> This the leavings of man's new wonders.

Here only petty thirsts, never for a universe,
By the shores of Dank and Dirty.
                                        —Trashcan O'Toole
                                        The Strip, 1964

Trashcan read what he had written, and watched the hot street. I'll bet that son-of-a-bitch Hiawatha never thought of Dank and Dirty, he thought.

TEN

It was 1:30 p.m., and Violet was waiting, too. Out of the city's thirty-odd car rental agencies, eleven had rented newly cleaned cars out on the night of Willie Mack's murder. Violet was waiting to see the man who owned the sixth agency he'd visited.

Violet was hot as hell. There was no other way to put it. It was hot as hell. Besides being hot, his stomach was rebelling against the not-so-hot lunch and the bad coffee he'd had after his fifth call.

Checking car agencies wasn't as bad as questioning whores, but it would never match up with a nice peaceful beat.

It was a bitch, Violet thought, how mostly people didn't trust cops. The cop on the corner who helped the kids across the street was a fine fellow. But put that same cop in a suit, and let him ask questions, then he wasn't such a fine fellow. He was a nosy son-of-a-bitch who must certainly resemble the M.V.D. That, or everybody in the goddamn city had a crime to conceal, judging by the way they acted. The first thing you learn as a kid is that cops represent the law. The second thing you learned was how to say, "I didn't do it."

There were lots of ways to say it. But it should be said before you knew what you didn't do that had made a cop show up in the first place.

The first one had said: "Cop, huh? I got nothing to hide."

Second was: "What is this all about? I run a legitimate business."

And next: "I'm clean. You want to look at my records?"

Then: "Look, I'm trying to make an *honest* buck. That bitch call you?" That bitch turned out to be an ex-wife who was on the receiving end of slow alimony payments. All of which Violet was not interested in.

Last had been: "Police!" Like he'd just heard of the second coming. "Police! Certainly, Officer, I certainly haven't anything to conceal from the police. Absolutely nothing!"

While he waited, Violet wondered how the next one would say it, and watched a tired-looking girl file her nails behind a desk in the corner. Business must be booming, Violet thought.

The agency's owner returned from lunch and looked at Violet. "Yes, sir," he said. "Can I help you, sir?"

"I'm from the police," Violet said, and showed him the panic button. "You had an earlier call from us."

The man watched him. "Can't understand it," he said. "I just can't understand what I've done wrong."

"Did you rent out a car last Monday night? One that had its upholstery cleaned that day?"

"It's against the law to clean a car?"

"Not that I know of," Violet said. "Did you?"

"I'll have to check the records on maintenance."

"What kind of upholstery cleaner do you use?"

"I'll have to check that, too. Does one of my rentals figure into a crime? I can't be held responsible for that, can I? I can't ask everyone that comes in here if they're going to commit a crime, can I?"

"Would you check your records, please?"

The man hurried off through a door marked MAINTE-NANCE. "Jesus Christ," Violet muttered.

"Sir?" the girl behind the desk asked.

"Just talking about someone I don't know," Violet said.

The girl watched him closely until the owner returned and waved some papers in his face.

"Here it is," he said. "This year's Buick. Did a quarterly cleaning on it—that's when we clean the upholstery, quarterly. We cleaned it in the morning and rented it out in the afternoon."

"Was it cleaned with Kar Klean? K's in the name instead of C's?"

"That's right. Maintenance crew swears by it. We clean all the cars with it, every three months. The Buick was due on last Monday."

"Who did you rent it to?" Violet asked, writing.

"C—P—L. Cecil P. Stone. C—P—L is corporal, isn't it?"

"How'd you get that?"

"Must have been rented on a military license. It's legal to rent to soldiers who have military licenses, you know. They always have the rank on them."

"Any address?"

"Let's see." The owner studied the writing. "All abbreviations. I can't make out what the hell they stand for."

"Let's see that." Violet read: Hq. & Hq. Co., 3d Recon. Bn., 2nd Army Comm. "Hell, that's Headquarters and Headquarters Company, Third Reconnaissance Battalion, Second Army Command."

Violet copied down the address. "License number? Where in hell is the license number?" He pointed to the blank space in the form.

The owner shrugged apologetically. "It should be there."

"It isn't," Violet said. "No service number, either."

"You want to talk to Acker? He's the one who checked this car out. I've got his home address."

"Yeah, I'll have to," Violet said. "I want to see the car, too, if it's in. We might need it for a while."

The car was in. Lonto wasn't, when Violet called the station. So Violet waited some more, until the men from the lab came over to pick up the Buick and let him go to make someone else nervous. He grinned slightly as he went.

Maybe Lonto's right, he thought. All we have to do is pick up Cecil P. Stone to find out.

The only trouble with that kind of thinking was that it wasn't going to be all that easy to pick up Cecil. It would seem a simple matter of calling the army base and locating the man there. That's how it might seem, but for one insignificant piece of information that Violet did ot have. Namely, that there was no Hq. & Hq. Co., 3d Recon. Bn., at the army base outside the city. There was not even a Second Army Command. It wasn't that someone had lost an army. It was just that a military driver's license did not need changing when a unit moved.

Violet was not aware that the simple matter of calling the base could develop into what Lonto called organized idiocy, which was his term for army procedure in finding a man. It would take a great deal of cooperation from organizations which had somehow got the impression that they were in competition with one another.

The C.I.A., F.B.I., M.P.'s, and probably the Provost Marshal would all have to cooperate, as well as several dozen officers and enlisted men. When they did, they would probably eventually find out just where in hell the Second Army Command was located, and then go down the line until they found out where Cpl.—no serial number—Cecil P. Stone was supposed to be. If said Cpl. did indeed exist.

If Violet had known this, and thought about it while he went to question Acker about blank spaces in forms and a possible description, he would have likely thought it was organized horseshit instead of organized idiocy—considering that nobody knew yet if Cpl. Cecil P. Stone had done anything to deserve all that attention. As it was, Violet thought about Acker, and the heat, and that being a detective was a lousy job no matter what you did. Being a detective wasn't what it was talked up to be.

Being a pimp wasn't what it was talked up to be, either. In fact, it was at present the most unpopular vocation on the Strip. For the first time since Silver Street became Pimps' Row, a stranger could walk from U.S. 28, down to Sixty-first Street, and cross the river to do the same up Jackson, without being offered the talented services of a number-one pimp. Nobody was a pimp, anymore. After the boost that the newspapers had given their fear even the whores were having a hard time finding their pimps.

As a result of the pimps' hiding, Silver Street was showing a bumper crop of whores who were displaying their wares as best they could with the advertising man of the team out of circulation. The beat cops sighed and shook their heads when five whores now worked a corner that had been the outside office of one pimp only a few days before. The beat cops could think of one good reason for pimps; they kept the whores off the street. The vice cops viewed the situation from another angle. They were doing a quick turnover of whore booking and a quick run of "taking it out in trade." It was a pleasant change from standing around the bus station washrooms, waiting for jock grabbers.

But too much of a good thing could become tiresome after a while. And, generally speaking, everybody on the Strip would just as soon see the pimps out of hiding and everything return to the frustrated routine, rather than the near-panic it was.

Dora Valdez hadn't panicked yet, but she was worried. She had spent the last two days looking for a pimp. She was also tired. It was hard work, looking for a pimp by day and looking for a trick by night. To say nothing of giving proper attention to Cecil, who took up the time in between the looking with other things besides sleep. Dora hadn't found a new pimp yet, and it was discouraging.

It was also discouraging that she had only twenty dol-

lars in her purse, since her weekly rent was due. Without
Pepe, she could not be absolutely sure that she could pay
the rent and find a trick tonight to pay for breakfast
tomorrow. Pepe, the bastard, had somehow managed to
see that she received at least one trick each night. But the
girls were now in open rivalry on the street, and Dora
could not compete with the young stock and be sure of
breakfast.

She could, if it came to that, ask Cecil for a token payment. A sort of wear-and-tear charge, or something. But
Cecil was her lover, not her trick. And lovers lasted
longer when they did not have to pay for their love. So
Dora elected to try to sneak past the landlady's room,
rather than pay the rent. Hell, she could pay the rent
tomorrow if she found a trick tonight. It wasn't that Dora
wanted to beat a rent payment; she wanted to postpone it.

Unfortunately, the landlady knew all about whores
postponing rent payments in favor of breakfast. It was
perhaps fortunate for the cops later, but it was unfortunate for Dora. The landlady's door was open when Dora
started by and heard the cackle from the room.

"Rent day, dearie."

The landlady's name was Mabel Claye. She was a
rusty-voiced, ancient hag of undetermined age, who
spent her time prowling the halls at all hours to discourage early morning check-outs.

"Oh, hello, Mabel," Dora sighed. "I was going to stop
this evening."

"Were you?" Mabel said. "I wanted to see you, dearie,
about your friend."

"He's just visiting," Dora said, and opened her purse.
"I have your money right here."

"All week he's been visiting!" Mabel shouted. "All

week! Whore, I told you before not to make my place a whorehouse!"

Dora held out the twenty-dollar bill. "That's my business."

"Mine! My business," Mabel screamed. "See the sign? 'Double occupancy of rooms—Twenty-five dollars a week.' Give me five more dollars or I call the police."

Dora shrugged. Maybe she could get it from Cecil. "This is all I have, you'll have to wait."

"Wait! For one hour I'll wait," Mabel said, taking the bill. "Make your friend pay. I'll wait one hour."

"I'll have your money before that," Dora said, turning to walk off.

"See that I do, dearie," Mabel said behind her.

Cecil was lying on the bed when Dora reached the room. His back was to the door, and he did not turn.

She put her empty purse down on the bed and sat down, reaching out to touch his shoulder. "Don't you care who's behind you?"

"I know you by your walk," he said. "I could find you in the dark by your sounds, and you'd never know I was there."

She kissed his neck. "Learn that over there? You move like a big cat."

"Yes," he said, turning onto his back. "I learned that over there. What was all the yelling about downstairs?"

"The landlady. Old bitch wanted her rent money." Dora moved her hands over his chest. "Five dollars more because of you."

"Take it out of my wallet," he said. "On the dresser."

She rested her head against his chest, listening to the muffled beat of his heart. "I hate to take your money," she said. "You're different than the others. I want to keep you here, forever."

"Don't be an ass," he said. "You'd take money from your pimp, wouldn't you?"

Dora didn't answer. He could feel her face, hot against his chest. "Wouldn't you?" he asked again.

She raised her head to look at his face. "That's different. With you it's different. I keep thinking . . ."

"That's good," he said. "What about?"

"About why you hate pimps. I keep thinking that when I read the newspapers. Someone else hates them, too, don't they? I wonder why you don't show any interest in that."

"Why should I?"

Her eyes were still on his face. "I don't know."

He laughed shortly. "Then don't think about it. I'm not interested in it. I'm over that, remember?"

"I remember," she said. "What did you do in the army, Cecil?"

He looked at her questioningly. "You're starting to sound like that cop you told me about. The pansy."

"Violet," she said. "His name was Violet."

"Violet—Pansy," he said. "You sound like him."

"I was just wondering," Dora said. "It doesn't matter, Cecil. I don't care anything about what you did. It's too good, just being with you."

He reached over, and took a cigarette from the package on the nightstand. "What do you think I did, that it doesn't matter?"

She stared at him, then she smiled a wise smile. "Nothing, just like I told that cop. I don't think. I don't know a thing."

He held her away, and sat up on the bed, letting his fingers unbutton the front of her blouse. There was a damp slick of sweat on his face. He could feel his chest become tight as his breathing quickened.

"Undress," he said, his fingers fumbling.

She held his hand against her breast. "You'd think it was your first time. Don't be so impatient," she laughed. "Where are you going?"

He crossed the room to his overseas bag. "Undress," he said. "I want to see you." He watched the white flesh unfold from the clothes as his hands found the cold steel of the knife. There was nothing else he could do, he thought. She might guess, if she hadn't already. His hands felt cold and his lips smiled as he wondered why he wanted it to be as good as killing a pimp was, when it was only a necessity.

Dora lay forked on the bed when she saw the knife. She licked her lips.

"What's that for?"

"You wanted to know what I did in the army," he said, breathing rapidly, as he watched a doubtful fear creep into her eyes. "I used this."

She pulled her eyes away from the knife as he sat down on the bed. "I don't care," she said. "Really, Cecil, I don't like knives."

"It's a beautiful knife," he said, holding it up. "A very special knife. See how it catches the light? We used to dirty the blade so they wouldn't give us away in the moonlight. I never liked to dirty my knife."

"Please, put it away, Cecil," she said, and raised herself on her elbows.

His face held her eyes. He gripped the knife lightly,

balancing it like a wand, with the point aimed at her. His arm inched forward.

"Right about there," he said. "On the left side. That's where I put it in the Army. That's where I put it in Pepe."

"Please . . ."

"In your pimp!" he said. "You know, don't you?"

"No! I don't know anything," Dora said, reaching out suddenly to touch his face desperately. "Put it away, Cecil, and come to . . ."

Cecil put it away.

His arm jumped forward, and Dora felt the blade inside her chest, like an electric shock. She fell back, and he let the knife remain, clinging below her breast like a metal leech. He watched her hands flutter weakly, and tug lightly at the hilt, and her lips almost calmly saying, "It hurts. Please take it out," before she died. Cecil left it in and pressed himself onto her.

Mabel came for her five dollars at 1:52 P.M. The beat bull heard her rusty-voiced screaming at two o'clock. Mabel had been screaming since she had entered Dora's room.

ELEVEN

AT THE STATION house, Violet and Lonto were catching each other up on what the day's sidewalk pounding had brought them, along with the heat.

"Anything on the car?" Lonto asked.

"Not yet," Violet said. "The lab's still working on it. This guy Acker couldn't remember the guy that rented it, either, not what he looked like, anyway. He said the guy picked up the license off the desk before he had a chance to write the number down. So he figured 'what the hell,' and left the place blank because they were busy. But we might get a break there. The Army promised a picture of the corporal. I'll check back with Acker when it gets here."

"If it does," Lonto said. "I was out there all morning. Three M.P.'s and I, on the phones, steady. Would you believe the only men with passes during the first night were general staff officers? Nobody was off base, not one swinging dick. A break of sorts."

"How come?"

"They were playing war games. Operation Sick Duck or some damn thing. We spent most of the time checking men on leave. They check out so far. Maybe I'm on the wrong track. Maybe he did learn knife fighting at finishing school."

"Maybe not," Violet said. "This corporal isn't from this base. We got that much. He was shipped out from here. Stands to reason he'd come back through here and be re-assigned, or discharged. Words of wisdom from the Provost Marshal."

"Now you're going to agree with me?"

"I think this corporal looks good," Violet said. "I'm getting a suspicious mind like you."

"Go ahead."

"Suppose you intended to kill someone, and were going to use a rented car? Suppose you didn't think about someone seeing the car until the last minute? That would make you pick up your license before the guy got any more off it than he had."

"Possible."

"We're assuming that Willie Mack was killed inside a car, or at least was inside of one. Then we might go along with your morbid line of thinking and say that being in the car was the reason he wasn't slashed, like Pepe Sanchez. This nut wouldn't want to turn in a car that looked like a slaughterhouse inside. So, he didn't play with Willie; he was being careful about blood. But he didn't know what the test tube wizards could do with the Kar Klean that Willie picked up."

"I think you have an evil mind, Violet," Lonto said. "The only trouble is that it could be like that."

"Using your theory of the same man on both cases it could," Violet admitted. "What makes an animal like that, Lonto? I'm a cop, but I don't know this kind of people. I can't tie the killings together for a reason."

"Maybe the newspapers did. They were both pimps."

"Coincidence?"

Lonto shrugged. "Something makes this guy kill pimps. If I knew what it was, we'd give Jaworski a killer. I wish that report on the car would get in; we need this corporal cleared, or in the slammer. Maybe we should drop down to the lab; nothing like standing around hopefully to make them speed it up."

The telephone rang on Wolverton's desk. Wolverton picked it up and growled in his usual good humor. Lonto and Violet watched each other silently. The one beat bull in the room developed a sudden urge to answer the call of nature, and headed for the can. Telephones are like that in a police station. When they ring, they give people the urge to be somewhere else, or to wait in reluctant silence. Telephone calls usually mean trouble.

"On the way," Wolverton said, when he was finished listening. "Right now," he added, and hung up. "Patrolman, on Fifth and Catcher. He's got another knifing. You two better take it."

"Oh, Jesus Christ! Not another pimp?" Lonto wanted to know.

"No." Wolverton handed over the sheet he'd been writing on. "Here's the address. I'll send the lab boys and the meat wagon. No hurry on them, he says she's dead."

As Violet had talked to few whores before, he had seen fewer dead ones. Dora Valdez made a total of one. He did not like the view. He liked being a detective even less than he had before he saw her. He saw the bleak room, with the floor showing through the rug, and the dirty windows, with the yellowed shades that were up to allow more light to view by.

Violet had a good view of the white body on the white sheet with the crimson splash over them both, as though an artist had painted an obscene red over a posing nude. It was a view that made him tremble inside. There was something entirely obscene about the mutilated nakedness of a woman in bed that did not attach itself to the viewing of a clothed body.

If Lonto felt the added obscenity, he gave no sign of it. He wiped his face in the heat and took notes while Violet began to puke in the small bathroom. The beat bull smiled blankly at Lonto, and went on talking.

"What's with him?" he wanted to know.

"Ulcers," Lonto said. "You talk to the landlady yet?"

"Talk! I couldn't shut her up. She's down in her apartment."

Lonto walked to the bed. "She was a hooker, you say?"

"One of the regulars. You people were down to talk to her a day or so ago—on the Sanchez killing. She was one of his hookers."

Violet was white and shamefaced in the doorway. "Yeah, I talked to her. Listen, you mind if I get some air?"

"You can talk to the landlady," Lonto said. "But take

107

a good look at her first. That the one you talked to?"

Violet looked at the body. "It's her, all right. She gave me a cup of coffee; she didn't tell me a damn thing, but she gave me a cup of coffee."

"See what you can get from the landlady," Lonto said. "You better see Doc about that ulcer, Ed."

"What, what . . . Oh, yeah, I will," Violet said. "Think this is our butcher, Tony?"

Lonto grunted. "Go get some questions answered," he said.

There were some questions that Frenchie Labiche wanted answered, too. One was, why does this son-of-a-bitch want to kill me over a floozie? It was very hard to believe that he already had the answer to that. It was all there in the envelope that Trashcan O'Toole had delivered. Six lousy words: READ THE NEWSPAPERS, PIMP. YOU'RE NEXT!, and there was the photo.

Frenchie's hands were sweating. He picked up the note and read it again. It made him remember the opium dealer in Hong Kong who'd welshed on a deal. Frenchie had sent him gold-plated cards, announcing his funeral, for six months before he had hired a killer to arrange it. It had given Frenchie hours of satisfaction to know how bug-eyed with fear the man had been, waiting. And now, Frenchie was waiting.

He removed the cork from the bottle on his desk and splashed whisky into his glass. He watched the note, like a snake on his desk, and tilted the glass up. It clicked against his teeth, spilling drops off his lips as he emptied it in two gasping swallows and slammed the glass back down. It didn't reach the cold knot of fear growing in his guts.

The picture of Tillie stared up at him from the desk. There was too much here to run. Too much going for him to get killed over a two-bit floozie. And he was back in her apartment, with her swinging in slow circles from the silk stocking she'd used. He wiped his hands on his trousers and opened the desk to take out his address book. There were fourteen men listed under Tillie's name who might want to kill him.

Which one was this son-of-a-bitch? Maybe I should go to the cops. Oh, baby, you'd really stick your foot in it then. They'd want to know all about that sweet little deal. It would be good for about five years in a crowbar hotel. That dago cop would laugh himself silly all the way to a cell if I took a fall for this guy. Me, Frenchie Labiche, copping a plea to get away from a nut! There's got to be a way out of this. Maybe I should mail the cops this list. No. They'd shitcan it as a crank.

Over a floozie! A goddamn floozie. What a life. Cops! And now I got to make a buck with this creep trying to kill me. A nut on my back.

Violet had Mabel Claye on his back, like a junkie's monkey. She'd been pounding his eardrums with her rusty voice from the second he'd come into her apartment.

"Cops!" she shouted. "Why do you ask me all this? You think I run a whorehouse here? I should know my tenant's business?"

"I know what you run here," Violet said. "Now shut up."

"What? . . . What?"

Violet leaned closer, and said it clear. "I said, Shut up!"

Mabel shut up.

Violet enjoyed the descending quiet, and folded back a page in his notebook. I wouldn't have done that in residential, he thought. I'm getting used to the slime, Papa. I'm not in residential; there's a dead girl upstairs.

"Now," Violet said. "We'll go through it again. I don't want to know what a tramp she was and what a fine, upstanding citizen you are. All I want is answers to my questions."

"Is this a police state? I pay taxes for you to talk to me like that in my own home?"

"Write the mayor about it," Violet said. "Just answer my questions now. You got that?"

"Police brutality. I've been hearing about it, but in my own . . ."

"What did this man look like?" Violet broke in with what he figured was a grilling tone.

Mabel thought it was. "He was a young man, maybe twenty or twenty-two. He was sickly-looking, I remember that. I thought he was too sickly-looking to be a soldier."

"How do you know he was?"

"The bag he carried. The kind that soldiers use. I saw it in her room."

"What kind that soldiers use? A duffel bag? A sea bag?"

"The kind they use to keep their uniforms from wrinkling," Mabel said. "I've had dozens of soldiers here, I never . . ." She stopped, seeing his face. "The kind that fold up to make a suitcase."

"What color were his eyes?"

"I didn't see them."

"You saw the suitcase."

"That's different. It was in her room."

"Did he wear a uniform?"

"Just dark slacks, and a dark shirt. I noticed that. They like the light color sportshirts in this weather. But he was always wearing dark clothes when I saw him."

"Did you notice any marks or scars on his face? Tattoos on his hands or arms?"

"No, dearie."

"How about his build? Heavy . . . ?"

"Dearie, he was sickly, and thin. I told you that."

"Hair?"

"Brown, I think. Light brown, and cut like those soldiers are supposed to wear it."

"Crew cut?"

"I guess so," Mabel said. "I was shocked that he would be interested in that tramp. So young and all. She was old enough . . ."

"Did you hear him talk? Hear his voice?"

"Well!" Mabel said. "How would I?"

"You'd find a way, I think," Violet said. "How was it? High? Deep?"

"Well, I only heard it once, when I was passing in the hall, dearie. It sounded high to me."

"Would you recognize him if you saw him again?"

"I wouldn't forget that one," Mabel said. "Not in a million years."

"Okay, good," Violet said. "That wasn't so hard to get over, was it? Sorry I said what I did. Have to get these things fast, no hysteria."

"I've never been hysterical in my life," Mabel said. "That's all?"

Violet folded his notebook. "Unless you remember anything more about today?"

"No."

"We'll check with you later," Violet said. "If you remember anything before I leave, just yell at the patrol-man on duty upstairs."

"Are you going to stop me from renting that room?"

"We'll let you know."

"I make my living from those rooms. What right do you have—"

"Write the mayor," Violet said.

He was going up the stairs when she yelled at him. "I'll report you if that room's left in a mess!"

Violet sighed.

The lab boys were making a mess of Dora's room. They were in no way interested in the room's appearance after they were finished with it. They only wanted to do their job and hand over a few facts that would hopefully land Dora's killer in the slammer. To do this, they made a mess.

It takes time to make a good mess by dusting for finger-prints in all the places there would conceivably be some. It was slow, laborious work. It made Lonto glad he was a detective rather than a lab technician.

And Dora's room had a lot of prints to make a mess with by dusting and transferring fingerprints to cellu-loid. Those that could not be transferred were photo-graphed, which was easier for the lab boys but still left a mess. The room looked a great deal like the battle-ground of a powder-puff war when they were finished collecting prints. They turned the prints over to the de-tectives who began to check them through police files. Lonto, being one of those detectives, sent the prints where he wanted them checked, which was with the C.I.A., the F.B.I., and the Military Records Department in Washington. Lonto wanted to know if any of the prints matched those of Corporal—no serial number—Cecil

Stone, if there was such a man. As far as Lonto knew, the combined cooperation of the military had not as yet found the Second Army Command. It did not surprise Lonto. It was organized idiocy, which to him was as painful as reading autopsy and lab reports.

While this was going on, the lab boys were collecting other prints and making a thorough mess. They collected footprints where they found them in the dust under the edge of the bed, and they collected what turned out to be a rump print, overlaid with Detective Violet's fingerprints from the toilet seat, which was never identified because of being overlaid. Then they collected hair. They also collected stains, and, to make sure that they didn't miss any bets, they cut pieces out of the rug and the sheets that were stained. Last, they vacuumed everything of importance, and collected the dust, before they carried the collection down to the lab in hopes of finding a small fact that might be helpful to the detectives.

They left the apartment in a mess. And nobody thought it was very important but Mabel Claye. Lonto did not think about it at all. He was down at the coroner's promoting speed with his hopeful presence.

The coroner had long ago recognized the detective as one who would remain waiting at the morgue until he received the information that he wanted. Everybody else waited for a report. Lonto didn't. If he did, he brought it with him when he came back to the morgue and demanded a course in the language of medicine. It was therefore best to reveal what was known, and preclude a second visit. It was also best because the girl's body had been given a priority tag.

"They are worried about this one," he said. "I shouldn't wonder, three knifings now."

"You think it's the same guy, Doc?" Lonto asked.

"I am not a detective," the coroner said. "I will leave that to you to decide. The same man, I wouldn't know. The same type of murder weapon, I'm sure of."

Lonto shook his head. "He broke his pattern," he said. "A girl this time. Two pimps and a hooker."

"And why do you think he did, Mr. Lonto?"

"I wish to God that I knew," Lonto said. "The girl was connected with one of the men, though."

"The girl was also raped," the coroner said tightly. "There is a very basic motive for you . . . But the cause of death was an extremely sharp, double-edged instrument, stabbed directly into the heart, as in the other two."

"All three of them." Lonto paused. "I wonder, Doc, would a layman know just where to stab for the heart like that?"

"As you said before, a man who knows a great deal about killing with a knife. A psychopath, do you think?"

Lonto smiled thinly. "I'll ask the psychoanalyst, Doc," he said. "I'm just supposed to catch him, not analyze him."

"Touché," the coroner said. "Each to our own trade. And if you don't mind, I'll get back to mine. It seems there are bodies waiting."

Lonto thanked him and left. It was seven o'clock, he was in possession of nothing helpful. He did not consider important the fact that the killer had added whores to his list of kills. Catching him was important.

There were a number of things waiting for him in the homicide office. One of them was Violet. Tony was beginning to have a dislike for a detective who acted like a rookie. He expected detectives to know something.

114

"We got a break, Tony," Violet said. "Lab report on the rented car. One of the prints from there matches some of those out of the girl's apartment. They lifted a print of Willie Mack's from the car, too. That's enough to hang the bastard."

"Fine," Lonto said. "Now, who do we hang?"

"Stone! Cecil Stone!"

"Prints match his, do they?"

"Okay, so they aren't back yet. We got something just as good. The Army came through with his records and a photo. He fits the description. And he's on leave."

"So do a thousand other guys fit that description. Have you checked the rest of it, or is fitting the description good enough now? How long has that information been here?"

"Since you went to the morgue."

"Then maybe you could have checked something in an hour. How about it? Did you?"

"No. I thought we were waiting for some leads."

"Yes. That's right. And what in hell are you supposed to be doing with those you already have? Have you checked if this guy is where he's supposed to be on leave? Have you even read his record? Or did that description wrap up the case for you?"

"Look, Lonto," Violet said, "I don't know what's biting you, but don't ride me. What the hell do you expect me to do? Check everything?"

"I'll tell you what's biting me. I expect you to pull your own weight when you work with me. I'm goddamn tired of you marking time and waiting for someone to tell you what to do. You're on the job, all right, but you don't do anything but make noise over what the rest of the men dig up."

"Is this because I got sick? You think I can't take it?"

"I don't give a damn if you puke every time you see blood. But, goddammit, do something when you're finished. Why'd I have to tell you to question the landlady? Why'd I have to get you the names and addresses of the whores we had to see? I can't be both ends of this team. Jaworski and the lab can't hold your hand and tell you what to do all of the time. Damn it, Ed. You're a cop. You're supposed to think and act like one."

"I was following orders."

"Fine," Lonto said. "But there's not going to be someone around to give them all of the time. That's what's biting me. You sat on this report and waited for me to tell you what to check. You should have checked it."

"I was doing my best!" Violet said. "If you don't want me on this, you can tell Jaworski to pull me off."

"You were doing nothing but coasting," Lonto said, "and you're not coasting with me. You're not taking the easy way out, either."

"I'm asking Jaworski to put me back on prowl car."

"You're going to finish this case first," Lonto said. "Then you can ask. Or I'll raise such a stink that you wind up pounding a beat on the Strip, where you should have started."

"What does that mean, Lonto?"

"You know what I mean. I want to know if coming up because you got connections makes the same kind of cop that working your way up does."

"I've been a good cop for a lot of years, Lonto. Just remember that. I got more years on the force than you."

"And you got connections?"

"If you say so."

"Then maybe you should wonder why I outrank you.

And maybe you should start using some of that experience you're supposed to have. Use some of it to check this guy out."

Violet was silent for a few minutes. "I'm going to check this mug shot with the Claye woman," he said finally, and walked out.

Lonto glared at the files on his desk.

Sergeant Wolverton came in with another file to add to the heap. Lonto glared some more.

"You're batting three hundred," Wolverton said. "Here's the last lab reports, and one from the F.B.I."

"How's that make . . ."

"And the Lieutenant wants you."

"Great," Lonto said.

"Sounded like you were initiating Violet in here," Wolverton said. "What was that all about?"

"Nothing."

Wolverton shook his head. "They don't make cops like they used to. This one's got stomach trouble."

"How's that?"

Wolverton paused at the door. "No guts, Tony. No guts. I'll tell the Lieutenant you'll be in."

TWELVE

ANNA RYAN sat at the window of her apartment and stared at the city. And while Wolverton prophesied the lack of guts in Violet, Anna wondered at her own. It had been very easy to let her body trap her into three more months with her pimp. It had also been easy to maneuver Lonto into confirming his feelings for her. All that remained to do was break with one and hold the other while she confessed her vocation to him.

But Anna did not care to proceed quite in that order. It was all very well to sacrifice the variation in her sex life for the doubtful privilege of raising blond dago kids, but it seemed entirely fair to keep her pimp until she had a husband. She would tell Tony Lonto tomorrow, because she had promised herself she would tell him during their third time in bed. And, if Mr. Lonto did not care for the facts, she would still have a job with her pimp. Love was a nice feeling to have, if that's what she had for Lonto, but it did not pay any bills or leave any opportunities for the future if it was taken away. If she had trapped herself into risking vocation for love, she rationalized that it was best to risk losing love first. One was a necessity, the other a luxury. If she might lose the cure for her perpetual hot pants, there seemed to be no reason to risk the source of a second-rate remedy as well.

She left the bedroom for the living room and waited there for Frenchie to arrive with the address of her trick for the night. She was also impatiently waiting for Frenchie's second-rate remedy, which she could view as part of her arrangement but not without a rising heat inside her. She wondered vaguely at the possibility that she could be, as Frenchie said, a little bit dyke as well as a large bit nympho. She did not spend a great deal of time with the thought.

Frenchie did not have time for trifling thoughts when he arrived at the apartment. At the moment, he did not care about whores, or tricks, or about making a buck, things that were usually foremost in his mind. He would care about them when he was sure that he'd be around to enjoy worrying about those minor problems. Right then, he was worried about the fact that someone intended to kill him.

The headlines in the newspapers were helping him do that. They read: KNIFE SLAYER KILLS AGAIN. WOMAN MURDERED. Woman, my ass, Frenchie thought. Two pimps

119

and a whore he's got. And he wants to make it three.

"Have you seen this?" he asked, and tossed the paper into Anna's lap. "Happened this afternoon."

Anna read for a moment before she said, "Look, Frenchie, if this guy's butchering women now, I'm staying off the streets."

"Your trick tonight is okay. I know him."

"Do you know he's not this killer?" Anna wanted to know. "I mean it. And I'm staying off the street."

"What did I say, bitch?"

Frenchie wasn't in the mood to argue with his whores. He took a quick step to where she sat, and caught the softness of her throat between thumb and strong fingers. She twisted, and slid out of the chair, pulling him down with her. She thrashed under him, and he avoided her hands as she raked at his face. There was a pleasure in the judicious mauling of a floozie that helped him forget his fear. She thrashed under his weight and then he sensed her struggling growing weaker.

Don't kill the bitch, he told himself. Just enough to show her who's boss. He released the pressure, sat back with her body under him, and smiled as she coughed and gagged for a time, then lay still, breathing hard.

"What did I say, bitch?" he asked.

"I'm not going . . ."

He rested his hand on her throat. "I said this guy's okay. I know he's not the killer."

"Know?" she whispered.

He had an impulse to tell her about the note and Tillie. To tell her and prove how brave he was.

"I could give the cops his name." He got off her, pulling her to her feet. "I got a love letter from him. He says I'm next."

She shivered, pressing her hand to her mouth. "My God. He might have followed you here."

"I'm not worried," he said. "He screws with me, and he'll wind up in the river. I'm telling you this because I don't want dissatisfied customers; they're bad for business. But I'm not worried. Keep that straight."

"If you know who he is, tell the police."

He laughed in a hard way. "I'll take care of my own troubles. Just remember that. It's my trouble, bitch. So don't go thinking you're going to use it to get out of tending to business."

She backed away from him. "It's not. It's not. That girl he killed. She was a prostitute. He isn't just after you. He's after all of us."

He advanced and pushed her down on the couch. "Shut up, or I'll beat the shit out of you."

"Touch me again and I'll scream my head off," she promised. "I'll have my boyfriend bury you in jail. He's a cop."

Frenchie stopped, watching her. So that's who was long-dicking him out of a good piece of trade. A goddamn cop! He felt a sudden urge to laugh.

"I'm not going to hit you," he said quickly. "I'm just trying to talk some sense into you."

The fear was back inside him. They were all trying to screw him up. Floozies, cops, that stinking punk killer. Every one of them. He rubbed his eyes. There had to be something to use against them. Something to play them off against one another.

Anna sat up on the couch, surer of herself now. He saw that in her. She knew her cop had stopped him for now. Watching her, he decided that her knowing a cop might help. She had some guts, but not enough to stand

121

up to him long. She could be twisted around to do what he wanted. Frenchie knew his whores.

"Maybe you're right," he said. "Maybe I should tip the cops."

She nodded.

"But there's a few problems there, sugar," he said. "Maybe your boyfriend can help with them. He should want to get this killer off the streets."

He sat down on the couch and ran his fingers over her flank. "I'll tell you about it, so you won't worry when you keep your date," he said, and smiled. "You will, sugar. I know you better than your boyfriend does."

She sat still as stone with fear and passion fighting in her eyes.

At 8:30 P.M., the day's heat was leaving the city. The reflecting glare of the sun no longer bounced off the sidewalks and buildings to try the city's patience.

And another type of heat was waiting to descend, in the form of newly printed police fliers. On the fliers was printed the picture of the man this heat was aimed at.

It was all in, the requested information from all the law enforcement agencies involved. The lab reports were in, each with PRIORITY stamped over its jacket. The coroner's report, and the police psychologist reports—everything was in but the killer. It was all in a pile on Lieutenant Jaworski's desk.

Violet and Lonto were in the office with brown-stained paper cups of coffee in their hands. They sipped at the coffee distractedly. They had been off duty since 4:00 P.M. The two relieving detectives were in the homicide details office conducting business as usual, but Lonto and Violet were not concerned with the fact that they were four and a half hours deep into a second shift. Breaks, like murders, do not adjust themselves to schedules. Cops adjust. They were listening to Jaworski outline his feelings.

"I want this bastard caught," he said, waving the printed flier in the air. "We got his fingerprints, we got his picture, and we got a positive identification from the Claye woman."

Lonto watched silently.

"We're getting the fliers out," Violet said. "Every patrolman, every car's getting them. The Strip, all this precinct, and we're putting them into the adjacent areas."

From outside the office, Lonto could hear the clicking of the teletype. He had written the message it was putting out:

SUSPECT WANTED FOR QUESTIONING CONNECTION THREE XXX REPEAT THREE XXX HOMICIDES XXX CECIL STONE XXX WHITE MALE XXX AGE 20 XXX HEIGHT 5′ 8″ XXX WEIGHT 130 XXX EYES HAZEL XXX HAIR LT BR XXX MILITARY CUT XXX SUSPECT MAY BE IN UNIFORM ARMY CORPORAL XXX LAST SEEN VICINITY 1642 CATCHER TWELVE THIRTY PM XXX SUSPECT ARMED DANGEROUS XXX CONTACT TONY LONTO DET 1G HOMICIDE DETAIL RIVER STATION.

There were several hundred cops in the city who would read the message and view the flier during the next hour. There were also a few million people for those cops to pick out the suspect from. It was a big city, but Lonto was concerned only with the Strip.

"You mean to tell me this guy can come in here and kill three people without you two knowing which precinct he's in? I've got twelve detectives and thirty-two patrolmen, and nobody's seen this guy?"

"Well . . ."

"This guy leaves prints around, and makes mistakes like a punk kid never would. He leaves a trail that an idiot could follow. I can't understand why he should be hard to find."

"We'll get him, Lieutenant," Lonto said. "We're asking the Army to pull in their passes. It'll cut down the number of soldiers in town."

"Have you come up with any reasons for this yet?" Jaworski asked. "We know the who's and the when's, but has anybody come up with a why yet? What's this guy's motive? It might narrow it down to where he'll try for the next one. If he does."

"He will," Lonto said.

"Tell me why," Jaworski said. He put the flier on the center of his desk and stared at the picture. He didn't like the face. Or to be exact, he didn't like the haircut. It reminded him of how Lonto looked when he had joined the force, fresh from the Army. That reminded him about how he felt about dagos, cops or not. It also made his ass hurt in the place he'd been trying to forget for twenty-some years. He looked at the man who constantly reminded him why it hurt, and asked questions because there was no getting around it that Lonto was a good cop. The best he had. It seemed like a deliberate slam from fate to make a dago his best cop.

"I had a talk with the head doctor," Lonto said. "It isn't that this guy wants to do his killing secretly and quietly and try to get away. He could do that by moving from city to city, and killing at random. He's not that kind of a nut."

"What kind is he?"

"Doc says he's got a reason. A motive that holds him

124

to killing a certain type. Maybe he kills for enjoyment, but he needs some way to justify the killings to himself, like maybe Jack the Ripper could justify his whore killing."

Jaworski shrugged. He didn't trust new police aids like police psychologists. "A nut. With or without a reason, he's doing it; we still got to catch him."

"We might not if Doc is wrong in his theory. He could just pack up and leave with all this heat on."

Violet nodded. "And start killing someplace else. Say cab drivers next time, or pick his victims at random. Just because he likes to kill."

"Yeah," Lonto said. "I'm hoping the Doc's right. I'm hoping that he's got his reason that keeps him where he can justify the killings to himself. It should be a pretty big reason that started this guy."

Violet was still smarting from Lonto's earlier ass-chewing. He wanted to justify something, too—the fact that he was a cop. He picked up the flier and studied the information listed. "You going to need me for a while?" he asked.

"Got an idea?" Jaworski wanted to know.

"I don't know. If Lonto's right, this reason might be big enough to have gotten some police attention. Maybe we already have his motive in our files."

"Well, where in hell do you start looking?"

"Pimps. A hooker. I'm going to start by borrowing the vice squad's files. Stone was at this base only for a few months. I think I'll check them from the time he got here until now. Maybe something will turn up."

Jaworski watched Violet go out and turned to Lonto. "I suppose you're going off duty?"

"Wrong." Lonto grinned. "I'm going to eat. Then I'm

going to talk to some stoolies on the Strip. *Then* I'm going off duty. I hope."

"Think he's still here, Lonto?" Jaworski asked. "Or will he run now?"

Lonto sighed. "He's still here. We wouldn't be so lucky to have him quit."

"Then let's get him," Jaworski said. "He's given us everything but a confession."

"Not quite," Lonto said. "He didn't give us his address."

THIRTEEN

THERE WERE NO new knifings on the Strip that night. And Lonto accepted this as a good omen in the morning. An omen of good luck that would follow him hopefully through the day to his date with Anna that night.

In the mornings Lonto was ready to love the world, even Jaworski. It was a short-lived feeling. It usually lasted until he reached the office and read the highlights that the graveyard shift had considered pertinent enough to note on the memo pad.

But, while it lasted, Lonto enjoyed it and let his thoughts wander over the things that brought a stir of pleasure in him. In his mind's eye he pictured Anna's bright hair as it had looked in the sunlight on the day he had met her in the park. She was a doll, all right, with those changing eyes and that grave pixie look of hers. He loved her, but he sensed that she was a woman he would never completely know or understand. And that made her all the more desirable.

He guessed that if she wanted to make him wait, it was just a part of being what she was. It made him jealous, too. But only because he wanted to know her fully and completely, to the last intimate detail of her life.

He pulled his car away from the curb, on his way to work, and smiled to himself. He hoped that his omen of good luck didn't follow the weather. It was dark and still with the low clouds spilling steady drops that usually meant a long dreary day of rain. He hated the rain. It made routine slower and paper work duller than it actually was. On rainy days he wished that he was a windowwasher, or a roofer, or some damn thing that would let him take every rainy day off.

Trashcan O'Toole thought he should take rainy days off, too. There was no profit to be made on rainy days. Even a newsstand needed the weather in its favor. But Trashcan had opened his shop as he always did. Business or not, the rain made a suitable setting for writing morbid poems about the Strip, which was exactly what he intended to do after he unwrapped the morning papers.

He knew just what he wanted to bastardize. He'd read it last night. "Charge of the Light Brigade," he thought. Already got the first two lines: Half a block, half a block, Half a block onward . . . Yeah, should be able to do something with that.

He thought about it while he put out the papers, wondering if Tennyson would recognize his poem after he was finished with it. Trashcan wondered also if anyone was going to recognize the man on the police flier that the beat bull had shoved into his paper box and asked him to put up. It was still in the box, he saw. He worked on his poem in his head while he pried a thumbtack out of the wall and then pulled the flier out of his box.

Trashcan forgot about his poem when he looked at the picture on the flier, and he quit wondering if anyone was going to recognize the man. The Light Brigade could wait. Cecil Stone, the name on the flier, couldn't. He hadn't, either, Trashcan remembered. He'd been in a hurry when he'd handed over the ten-spot to get a letter delivered to Labiche.

"Jesus," Trashcan said thoughtfully. He was a man who was very careful about offering information to the police. What could you get from cops but a reputation for talking to cops? Trashcan lived by the four punk's rules that were necessarily followed to ensure health on the Strip. The punks said that you drank a lot of water, walked slow, carried a big stick, and you didn't talk to cops. If you did, there would be some loud talking, some fast cutting, followed by some sad singing and some deep digging. There was a bundle of wisdom in that, Trashcan thought. He did not honestly care to help the police. But he had eaten a five-dollar supper the other night on police money. Talking to Tony Lonto wasn't really talking to the police. He liked Lonto. He did not like Wolverton, who answered the phone when he called the station.

"Put me through to Lonto, will you?" Trashcan asked.

"He's busy. What do you want?"

"I want Lonto," Trashcan said. "You the chief censor around there?"

"Either you go peddle your newspapers or tell me why," Wolverton growled. "I got no time to argue with you."

"It's about the flier—the killer," Trashcan said.

Lonto had been at his desk for fifteen minutes when the telephone rang. Long enough to read the bleak highlights of the night's doings and for his love for the world to wear thin. Violet had not reported in yet, either. So Lonto resented the telephone's insistent ringing. He lifted the receiver and said, "Lonto, homicide to insecticide, you name it, and I get it. What's up, Wolverton?"

"You. It sounds like," Wolverton said. "You got a bottle in there, Lonto?"

"I wish I had. I'd get soused to the hair roots, and I wouldn't need to worry about homicides or insecticides."

"Oh, fine. I'll send one up. You feel like doing some listening, or do you want to dream up some pink elephants to go with the drunk?"

"Spiders," Lonto said. "I get spiders. I got soused for three days in Japan once and had a pet spider for a week before he went away. That saki is a bitch."

"Okay. Sure. I'll tell this guy to call back when the drunk is over."

"It's never over," Lonto said. "Always planned. What've you got, Sarge?"

"I got O'Toole on the line for you. Says it's about the knife killer."

"All right, put him on."

He waited. In a moment, Trashcan's voice came onto the line.

"Tony?"

"Yeah. You pick up something?"

"I don't know if it'll help. I just got a look at the flier you guys put out."

"You know the guy?"

"I delivered a message for him. That's all I know about him," Trashcan said. "He stopped at my place and gave me ten to deliver it. A envelope with nothing on it."

Lonto waited. His hands were sweating. "Who was it to, Trashcan?"

"Labiche—Frenchie Labiche."

"A tail on Labiche!" Jaworski demanded. "What in Jesus Christ for?"

"Just put on a man watching his bar," Lonto said. "Violet can pick him up and tail him from his apartment. He's connected with this killer somehow."

Jaworski picked up the phone and talked a moment. "What's the connection?"

"I'll tell you later, when I find out," Lonto said. "Soon as I read some vice squad files, maybe. He might be on the schedule as the next pimp dead. He'd never tell us, you know."

"We could use a break like that," Jaworski said. "Live bait for the pimp killer. Check it out and let me know. Violet was in there until midnight last night, and all he got was eyestrain."

"All I want is Labiche's file," Lonto said, and went out into the hall. Violet was coming out of the office.

"What's up?"

"Maybe a break," Lonto said. "Come on and we'll read some more pornography while I fill you in."

"Not the vice files!" Violet said. "I'll go blind. My mind will rot."

131

"We'll risk it," Lonto said. "But I'll do the reading. I want you to start watching this guy as soon as we get his address and you can get over there. I'd take it myself, but he knows me."

"What is he?"

Lonto grinned. "He just might be our next murder."

Violet was silent. He took the home address of Frenchie Labiche that Lonto found in the records and went thoughtfully out into the rain. He wondered why his service revolver seemed suddenly to have gained weight and pressed heavy against his stomach.

Peter Krumrey was a vice cop. He'd been on the vice squad since he'd been promoted off a beat. There was nothing he liked better than pinching whores and fairies. He was a frail-looking man with glasses who looked like a trick. After seven years of peeping through keyholes and breaking down bedroom doors, he found that his own sex life had become almost Victorian and quite static, much to his wife's disgust. It was not his sex life that was troubling Krumrey.

"Labiche? Labiche? You can't put a tail on Labiche."

"The hell I can't," Lonto said, reading. "Why can't I?"

"We've been working on him for months," Krumrey said. "If he spots a tail, we can kiss him good-by. We almost got enough for a pinch."

"You can maybe kiss him good-by if he doesn't get a tail. We're not after him. We hope someone else is." He looked up from the file. "Why all the interest in him? Anything I can use?"

Krumrey wrung his hands. "You know we've been trying to break his call-girl racket since we connected him with that suicide—you were in on that, weren't you? The Bolite girl?"

"I answered the beef," Lonto said. "It was a suicide. Homicide or suicide, I get them down there."

"Ummm, yes. Well, we found out she had worked for Labiche. We were getting some pressure from uptown to clean up the call girls. Seems that this Labiche was working the Bolite girl on the servicemen. That's where the pressure came from originally. Five G.I.'s applied to the Red Cross for an emergency leave to attend their fiancée's funeral. All the same girl."

Lonto tapped the file before him. "How come it's not in here? Big secret or something?"

Krumrey licked his lips. "I keep the currents in my desk," he said. "Anyway, it figured out that Labiche was using her to milk these boys out of their combat pay every month. She had love letters all over her apartment. Fourteen different guys. All overseas."

Lonto sat and stared out the window at the rain for several minutes before he said quietly, "Pete, would you kindly check that secret file in your desk, and see if a Corporal Cecil Stone is one of the guys she had going."

"Is it important?"

"Nothing to trouble the vice squad about, Petey boy," Lonto said. "It just might be a motive for a murder."

Krumrey agreed that it was a very good motive after they found Cecil's name. "That's what Violet was looking for, huh?" he asked. "Never thought to tell him about the currents in my desk."

"He was looking for something like that, I think," Lonto said.

"Well, I always keep the currents in my desk. I didn't think it would matter. I like them handy . . ."

"Okay! Okay! I know all about the currents. What else have you got on Labiche?"

"It's a policeman's dream," Krumrey said. "We have

the names and dates of almost every business transaction his girls held during the last two months. We're ready to fall on him, Lonto. We even have the girls' names—fifteen of them."

"We'll try not to mess up your game," Lonto said. "I've got to put a tail on him, Pete. He might give us a killer."

Krumrey sighed. "I suppose you'll want the girls' names and addresses, too?"

"I don't think . . . Yeah, you'd better give them to me. Labiche could be at any one of them." Lonto paused. "Holy Christ. Why'd you let me send Violet out? We got to find out which shack-up he's at before we can tail him."

"Well, I didn't . . ."

"Never mind," Lonto said. "Give me the names, and tell Jaworski about this. How'd you get all this crap? Tapping wires?"

Krumrey grinned. "Better than that. We've got a stoolie working for him. His day bartender. All he does is pick up the bar phone and listen in while he writes it down for us. It is really ready to fall on him . . ."

"If he's around to fall on," Lonto said. "Let's have your list, Pete. I'll check them myself and leave Violet watching the apartment."

"It seems like such a waste," Krumrey said, going to his desk. "Fifteen at one shot. Nobody's ever pinched fifteen at once before, unless it was a house."

"Yeah," Lonto said. "You won't get a medal for whore pinching this year. Maybe they'll give you one for fairy killing."

Krumrey had a pained expression on his face when he handed Lonto the list.

FOURTEEN

BETWEEN THE POLICE station on the corner of Twelfth and Olson and Frenchie Labiche's apartment on Wipply there is a park. As parks go it is no great shakes. If you spent a determined day within its boundaries, you could possibly count every one of the tired-looking trees that always seemed slightly wilted because of the city's dirt that hung on the leaves in a greasy coat.

But it was a park. And most of those who visited it did not notice the wilted look or had forgotten what a fresh green tree looked like. The park contained a small pond that was surrounded by worn-out grass and tired-looking bushes to match the trees. There was also a statue of a forgotten hero at the park's center where the paths met in a benched circle and old men came to sit and feed the pigeons.

So, it was a park. And when you remember a place like that, where you liked to go as a kid, you usually remembered it when you needed some place to go as an adult.

Tony Lonto sat on a bench by the pond. It was a strange day to sit in the park. The rain was falling in a cold steadiness that made the trees weep each time a stray gust of wind touched the branches. The sky was black as the metal statue standing alone without its aging guards. And the one bird in sight was a bedraggled-looking sparrow that chirped bitterly from its perch in the low branches of a shrub. There were no other sounds but the hiss of car tires on the wet streets and the distant rumble of thunder.

Lonto sat on the bench with his legs spread, his hands folded and hanging between them, his body resting on his elbows in a slump. He listened to the rain play its pygmy chant on the pond and on the tight back of his raincoat. He was in the park on a strange day for a strange reason for a cop. His thoughts were also strange for a cop. He was thinking how pleasant it would be to remain where he was until a killer found another man, without police interference.

Tony Lonto sat with his thoughts and silently added his own tears to the drops falling on the crumpled paper on the ground between his feet. Anna Ryan's name was the sixth one on the vice squad's list of Frenchie's whores. It did not seem strange to Lonto that he should weep in the park in the rain.

He had read and rejected Anna's name on the list as

a mistake. Anna a whore? he had asked himself. The woman I want to marry—a hooker? A flat-on-her-back, legs-up-for-money whore? No. It was a mistake. But he was too much a cop not to realize that Krumrey had the patience of a wall when he investigated. He could not ignore the creeping facts that screamed at him from his mind. Anna's odd working-hours were decidedly clear now.

He would confront Anna with these facts, and he would talk logically and sensibly. It did not seem such a large crime that his fallen angel was a whore. It was the crime of allowing himself to love her, without knowing, that loomed large in his mind. There was a terrible emptiness in his chest when he realized that his love had been spent on one of Frenchie Labiche's whores. And Lonto despised Labiche.

He did not hate. For hate was an emotion that he reserved inside himself. Like love, hating must be done totally and completely. There were no petty shades of hatred in Tony Lonto. His character demanded that he hate as openly and as honestly as he loved. He did not feel that kind of hatred for Labiche.

And so he finished with his thoughts in the park and felt himself somehow guilty of loving and contaminated with the idea that he had dirtied himself by sitting in the park and hoping that his delay would allow a man to die. But he could not find in the new emptiness inside the answers that would help him face Anna with the truths that being a cop had brought him.

He had chosen to be a cop, and he condemned the job that presented him with facts that were no less ugly because they had suddenly become personal. But he was honest enough not to blame the job for the mirror world he had built around Anna. He left the park, walking heavy with a damp and wrinkled paper in his pocket, and he cursed the stupidness that had let him walk blindfolded into this.

It was 10:00 A.M. when the beat bull came up to Violet, who was watching the car belonging to Frenchie Labiche. The car was parked against the curb in front of an apartment building and Violet watched it through the rain-streaked windows of his own car. The beat bull tapped his nightstick against the car's window and waited patiently, looking like a huge bat in his raincape, as Violet rolled down the window.

"You Violet?" he asked. "I'm Packer. I got a message from the Lieutenant."

"Uh huh," Violet said. "What is it?"

"I got it wrote down. Seems the vice squad passed this on to your partner and Jaworski wants to know if it's being checked."

"What checked? You lost me, Packer."

"Where this Labiche is at."

Violet leaned forward and looked up the street. "He's in his apartment. Car's still there."

"That one?" Packer asked. "The blue Ford?"

"Yeah."

"If that's Labiche's, he's not in that apartment," Packer said. "I saw him park it and get in a cab about nine-thirty. Thought it was funny he took a cab and left his own car."

"Goddammit, the landlord said he was in," Violet said. "Said he'd heard him come in last night."

"Well, he ain't," Packer said. "I remember the guy because he usually comes out of there about the same time I get off shift, at noon. He's going to work and I'm getting off."

"Are you sure?"

"Positive." Packer paused. "Want I should ring the Lieutenant? He sounded kind of impatient." He paused again and looked carefully around the street. "Where in hell is your partner, anyway? He out checking these names?"

Violet took the list from Packer's hands. There was an urge to call the station and ask the Lieutenant what to do. "Jesus," he said. "These are Labiche's girlfriends?"

Packer shrugged. "Places he might be at, the Lieutenant said. How about it? What should I call in?"

Violet wore a puzzled expression. He took a deep breath and said, "Tell him Lonto's checking one end of these, and I'm starting on the other. And tell him we haven't spotted Labiche yet. Goddamn landlord."

Packer started off.

"Keep your eye on that car," Violet called. "And call in if Labiche shows up."

This guy must be Casanova, he said to himself. He wondered about that. He hoped that the killer was having as hard a time finding Labiche as they were.

As Violet had guessed, Lonto was checking Frenchie's list of whores. By 11:00 A.M., he had reached the sixth name on the list. In his heart, he was hoping that Krumrey had for once made a mistake in his bedroom snooping.

Anna was still in her pajamas with a housecoat over them when she answered the door. She looked tousled and warm, and beautiful. But she remained alien to Lonto's eyes.

"Tony?" The voice was warm with surprise.

"Can I come in?"

She held the door open and smiled. "Coffee break?"

"No."

"Don't tell me you've taken the day off?" Anna said. Her voice sounded clear and promising, and somehow it didn't fit her any longer.

"No," Lonto said again. "I'm here on business."

"Business?" Lonto watched her, watched for the expression to change, for the eyes to become hooded.

"Where's Labiche, Anna?" he asked. He waited, feeling his mouth go dry, watching for the wonder that he hoped would show in her face. Telling himself it could be a lie, a mistake.

"Labiche?" she said slowly. "I don't know anyone by that name, Tony. Is this a joke?"

Lonto watched the lips form the lie, and it ate away inside him until it reached the cop. And he reacted like he would as a cop questioning a hustler with a new homicide at stake.

"Nicholas Labiche," he said. "Frenchie to his girls. Where's Frenchie at?"

"Just what is this?"

"Goddammit, Anna!" he said. "Don't lie to me anymore! I know you're one of his hookers."

"How did you . . ."

"Never mind how," Lonto said tightly. "Where is Labiche?"

"Oh, stop acting like a cop!" she flared. "You didn't expect a virgin, did you?"

"I *am* a goddamn cop!" Lonto said. "And I didn't expect a virgin. I didn't expect a whore, either."

"Don't you dare say it like . . . like something filthy!"

she said. "I didn't lie to you. I didn't promise you anything."

He kept his voice under control. "All right. We'll go down to the stationhouse, and you can tell the vice cops where he is."

She stepped back with her hand to her mouth. Her eyes wide. "You would?" she asked.

"I will," he said. "I haven't got time to play games with you because you know me too good. I'm doing you a favor by tipping you now, anyway. I'll give you to the vice squad, Anna."

"But, Tony, you can't. Not after what we've been to each other. I would have told you about it before . . . You can't."

"Like hell I can't."

She took a long trembling breath. "You don't care at all? You don't love me?"

He grabbed her and shook her. "Will you get it through your head that this hasn't anything to do with us! I'm trying to stop a murder, Anna!" He held her at arm's length and looked at her. "I'm telling you there's a fall coming if you stay here. I don't have to do that. Now, where's Labiche? Was he here last night?"

"Yes," she whispered. "He wanted me to give you the names of the men who might be after him. But you already knew—the newspapers had his picture in it."

"He was here all night?"

"I was out for a while."

His mouth twisted. "On a trick?" he asked.

She looked away from him.

"It doesn't matter." He went on, "Was he here the rest of the night, then?"

"Yes."

141

"Then where is he, Anna?"

"He left this morning about nine." She paused. "I think he went to his apartment."

Lonto let his hands drop from her shoulders. "He's covered, then," he said. "The stinking bastard's got a cop protecting his rotten ass."

He looked at her and down at his hands. There didn't seem to be anything more to say. "I guess that's it, then," he said.

She stopped him at the door with her voice. "It could have worked, Tony. I would have told you tonight. I . . ."

"Save it," he said, shaking his head. "You'd better move, Anna."

"The vice cops?" she asked. "Tony, you could fix that, we could still . . ." She let the rest trail off and stared at the empty doorway.

And she stood there silently for a long time, listening to the steps fade down the stairwell, before she went to the bedroom and pulled her suitcase from the closet. She thought about the fifty dollars in her purse—last night's trick. She thought about the next city. She thought about Frenchie Labiche and the crazy guy who wanted to kill him.

Anna thought about being one jump ahead of the vice cops again, and she couldn't keep Tony Lonto out of her mind while she packed.

He would have understood, she told herself, and began to cry—hopelessly, helplessly—for herself, and what she couldn't control inside her.

FIFTEEN

Tony lonto stood in the building's entrance alcove, just inside the glass door, and watched the rain with veiled eyes. He's covered, he thought. The slimy, evil bastard is covered.

And why should you sweat it, Lonto? he asked himself. Did you think that half an hour in the park would make the difference? Or did you hope it would? Thirty minutes for the killer to get to him. A wasted thirty minutes. You wasted a lot of them before, so why sweat these? He's covered. Protected. And there's no one in the world who would begrudge you that thirty minutes. . . . You can't wake up nights dreaming something inside you

143

let a homicide take place when you weren't trying to stop it.

It's raining like a bitch, he noticed. Okay. You did your job. You found out what you had to. You're a hero! With a little more luck you'll get a killer today, or tomorrow, or whenever he comes for Labiche. You can't even say it was a crime to tip Anna. A cop is expected to pay for his information. So, you paid for it. You did her a favor. So, goddamn the vice squad!

He wiped a hand over his eyes, and stared at the names on the mail slots in the wall. Anna. Anna, he thought. He was studying her name when the door clicked and Violet's voice said, "You see this Anna Ryan?"

Lonto looked up, startled.

Violet held a list like Lonto's in his hand. "I started at the bottom and worked up. Knew I'd meet you somewhere. You check this Anna Ryan?"

Lonto's jaw worked silently for a moment. "I checked her," he said. "Who's watching Labiche?"

"He's not in his apartment," Violet told him. "Jaworski got impatient and buzzed a call box with this list." He paused and grinned. "Patrolman delivered it and said he'd seen Labiche go out before I got there, so I started checking these. Funny, though, the landlord said he was in."

"That son-of-a-bitch," Lonto said flatly. "Where's that bastard at?"

"What's with these dolls?" Violet asked. "I want to tell you, I've seen some dishes this morning."

"Whores," Lonto said. "His stable." He jerked his thumb over his shoulder. "He spent the night here, left about nine."

"That checks. He left his car at his apartment just after that. Took a cab off somewhere."

Lonto shook his head. "We better put an A.P.B. on him," he said. "We can't cover him unless we find him."

"It'll blow it," Violet said, "if this killer's watching him."

"It'll keep him alive. That's our job."

They went out into the rain. "Nothing on Stone yet, either," Violet said. "Every cop in the city is looking. Not a peep. Where'd he go?"

"He crawled into a hole. All the heat made him hide." Lonto stopped. "Why is he in? Why did he say he was in?"

"Who?" Violet stared. "What?"

"The landlord. Jesus Christ. He told you Labiche was in his room! Why? How'd he know?"

"He heard him come in," Violet said. "He heard . . . last night. He was here last night?"

"Upstairs with Anna Ryan," Lonto said, and his glance went briefly to the building. "Goddammit, Violet. Stone! He heard Stone! He's waiting for Labiche to come home. We can't find him if he's been in that apartment since the fliers went out."

And Lonto was pounding down the wet sidewalk toward his car.

In the apartment on Wipply, Cecil waited calmly and wished that he dared turn on the radio again. But that might give him away. He could not be caught until Labiche was dead. They had certainly figured out the rest. That is what happened when you underestimated people. He thought about Dora with a sudden sadness. They would understand the pimps, of course—the newspapers and the police, who had made it so difficult by using his picture. They would understand after Labiche. But it would be difficult to explain Dora. It was a thing he'd had to do. Couldn't they see that?

Perhaps not. It would be better not to be caught and let them wonder. He should care about that. He should really care about that more than he did the knife. But the excitement of being hunted added to the kill. As fear did.

He smiled in the grayness of the room. That was a good idea to make the pimp feel the fear. Make him know why he was dying. Would the police know? He doubted it. Afterwards they might, but not yet.

He stopped his thoughts at the sound of the door slamming one floor below him.

He reached into his shirt and his hand closed on the knife. It glittered like silver in his hand. This helped, too, he thought. Waiting for the door to open. Waiting, like he'd learned to wait. The expectancy with the knife in his hand. And soon the door would open.

He waited behind the door.

This time. This time. The footsteps came up the stairs.

The beat bull told them Frenchie was home, and the mailbox downstairs wore his name under 212. Lonto took the steps two at a time, holding his revolver in his hand when he reached the second floor.

Because it was entirely possible that he was about to make an ass out of himself by kicking in a door to find only a domestic scene, if there was anything domestic about Frenchie Labiche, and because Violet was pounding up the stairs at a slower rate—which might be laid to his physical condition or to his prophesied lack of guts —Lonto's kicking in of Frenchie's door was an individual act.

He kicked it twice, flat-footed kicks, aimed at the latch and launched from the wall opposite the door. The lock sprung and carried him into the room on the second kick.

While Lonto was prepared for the prospect of making an ass of himself and finding Frenchie calmly reading or such, he was also prepared to find a killer. But one does not expect to find bodies lying on the floor where self-propelled policemen can stumble over them. And Lonto saw the pale-looking man standing across the room with a small automatic in his hand as he crashed to the floor with the warm body of Frenchie tangling his legs.

He felt ridiculous, throwing out his hands to break his fall, when one of those hands held his pistol. He wanted to shoot, and roll, and shout at the same time, and only managed a warning, as the automatic spit across the room at him.

In the split second Violet viewed the scene, it was exposed in detail on his mind. He would remember later that the man was smiling as he held his arm extended toward the two men on the floor. He would remember that the man seemed to be aiming the pistol with precision slowness, as though the universe had stopped, and there was nothing so important as sending a bullet into the sprawled form of Lonto.

Violet did not have time to be sick with the thought. He fired automatically. He fired with his arm locked into his side, as he did on the police range. He placed the shot just where the nine-circle appeared on a silhouette target, slightly off-center at the top of the man's chest.

147

The automatic in the man's hand jerked and boomed at the same moment, but Violet's slug was driving him back against the wall with his knees folding under him. The man gripped the automatic in both hands as Violet crouched into the room. He wore the same smile as he fought to bring the gun on Lonto again.

"Drop it, you son-of-a-bitch! Please drop it!" Violet watched the gun fight its way up, and fired again.

His bullet struck the man in the left eye, making something bat-like and dark fly away from the back of his head and cling to the cracked plaster on the wall. And Violet was finished shooting, because the choking rush of sickness limped his arm and bent him retching on the floor.

Lonto was up and at his side.

"Easy, Ed," he said. "You got him. You got him."

Violet fought the sickness and the shock grabbing at his mind. He stood in the room with its smell of blood and the pressing sense of death in the air, and he sucked deep ragged breaths as he looked.

Then he began to shiver and mumble. "I'm a cop, Papa. See? I'm a cop, Papa."

Lonto patted his shoulder without speaking.

SIXTEEN

It CONTINUED to rain throughout the afternoon. It made a sober background for the rejoicing being done in various parts of the city.

The pimps on the Strip read the newspapers with widening smiles and telephoned their whores with an eagerness to return to work. The beat bulls sighed and drew creased fliers from their jackets to deposit into trashcans or gutters.

It was finished. The facts were in. A man had killed, and, in turn, had been killed. The reports were made and the bodies tagged on cold stone slabs in the morgue. The city read the sterile facts and went back to the business of living. It was simply and clearly reported. There had been a festering sore and the police had removed it from the city's face, as it was their job to do. It was an ending. Few wondered how it began, and whom it touched before it had ended.

Ed Violet went home to his wife with a new shadow in his eyes. He did not feel like a brave man who had faced a killer. He felt only a deep, bitter resentment, and a loss of something, but he could not guess at what it was. He knew only that he had lost it doing a job he had himself chosen to do. Yet, he managed to rejoice with his fellow officers that it was done.

But for Tony Lonto it was not finished. He left the station and walked in the rain to the diner on the corner. To him, it was not finished because it had not started here in this city, or on the Strip. Or in any of the cities with places like the Strip. You did not finish a thing by stamping white manila CASE CLOSED in red ink. It was never finished, when it had no beginning, except in the minds of men where it lurked and waited for the right environment to feed its growth.

So Lonto asked silently that it not rise again like a phoenix and begin where he had to deal with it. Tomorrow he would be all right, but he would like now to just sit by himself, and maybe have a few drinks to help him forget people and the things they did. Maybe to have a few more, to help him forget Anna, along with the knowledge that there was an evil being born, growing, or ending while he walked, and not any of the three could be truly finished.

So he settled for coffee, rather than the drinks, while he thought. He did not recognize the waitress until she placed the cup on his table.

"Hello, cop," she said.

"Hello, Trixie," he said, surprised.

She blushed as though the white of a waitress uniform was a chastity belt.

"It's just Helen now," she said. "The other is finished."

Maybe, Lonto thought. Maybe it is. He smiled thinly at the girl and watched the figure of Wolverton hurry past the wet windows to the door. "Helen, then," he said. "It sounds better."

Wolverton wore a lopsided grin as he stepped through the door. "Lieutenant wants you, Lonto," he said. "Trouble on the Strip."

Lonto winked at the girl, and dropped a quarter beside his cup. "There usually is," he said. "But it works out, sometimes."

He went out with Wolverton under a sky that promised more rain and listened to how cops were during the "good old days." As he walked he pulled up his collar against the wind that whipped into the city from the north.

About the Author

E. Richard Johnson was born in Prentice, Wisconsin, in 1937. He attended Phillips High School, which he left before graduation to enter military service. He served in the Army, both in the United States and in Europe from 1956 to 1960. He completed his high school education while in the service.

At various times Mr. Johnson has worked at logging, forest work for the Department of Agriculture, worked on well-drilling rigs, as a powder monkey, and as a ranch hand—never staying "in one place longer than the time it took to collect enough money to go on the bum again."

Mr. Johnson is presently an inmate of the State Prison at Stillwater, Minnesota.